CHARLIE'S QUEST

GRADY BRYANT

ALSO BY GRADY BRYANT

Roswell One the final contact

The Devils Bible the lost tablets

Drag Race Fever

Match Race Madness

Visions of Hell

HARLEY BOYS SERIES

The Gold Bar

The Swamp Ghost Mystery

The Wolf Pace Mystery

This story is fiction: however, the events represented in this story are based on true accounts.

First PrintingManufactured in the United States of America All rights reservedCopyright 2020 by Grady Bryant. This book may not be reproduced in whole or in part, by mimeograph or any other means, without permission. http://gradybryant.net

Printed by CreateSpace, An Amazon.com Company

Available from Amazon.com and other book stores

Available on Kindle and other devices

ISBN-9798643293378

CHARLIE'S QUEST

Proverbs 16:31
Gray hair is a crown of glory; it is gained in a righteous life

Psalm 71:9
Do not cast me off in the time of old age; forsake me not when my strength is spent

CHAPTER ONE

The sound of a Harley Motorcycle rattled the windows of the Deming, New Mexico nursing home, where Charlie Wise now called his home. Gone were the days when his wife called him to breakfast and the smell of coffee filled the air. His world was now a small lonely room with a single bed. The walls were lined with pictures from the past, of Charlie, his wife and their two sons. They were all gone now, and the only ones in Charlies life were the people in this nursing home. Most of them were good caring women who he trusted and shared his thoughts with. Some were only counting the hours until the day was over and they could do the things that young people do. Charlie had heard them talk about the parties and wild things they did over the week end. Charlie would just shake his head and walk away from their conversation, he couldn't believe the people of this day compared to the young people of his time.

Charlies dress consisted of a long sleeve shirt, buttoned at the neck and a pair of faded jeans. He had finally given up wearing his boots and gave in to the slip-on house shoe, but today was his day to clean up the offices in one of the few office buildings in Deming. It's close enough for Charlie to walk and he wore his boots instead of his slip ons. It wasn't much of a job, but it gave Charlie some extra spending money. The owner of the building always paid Charlie in cash, which made him feel good. It reminded him of the by gone days when he always had a pocket full of greenbacks to spend.

"Charlie, have you heard anything about my new piano. I need it for my next recital," said a frail voice from the hall way.

Charlie slowly shook his head side to side at the confusion of some of the people in this home. He opened the door and an elderly woman in a wheel chair was resting in the door way.

"Charlie, they were to deliver it

yesterday. Will you check on it for me, please?"

"I'll do it first thing, Dottie. Now go on down to dinner and I'll join you later."

The old woman turned her chair and wheeled away down the hall, leaving Charlie standing in the door way with a smile. He thought to himself that woman has been waiting for the piano to be delivered for years and I doubt if she can even play the piano. Some of the people here lived in their own little dream world. As Charlie walked down the hallway he met old man Bennie who grabbed his arm in a panic.

"Charlie, you seen my caddy? I have an important meeting down town this morning and I can't find it anywhere. I don't remember where I parked it. Can you help me find it?"

Charlie took hold of old man Bennies arm and helped him back to his room. Charlie guided him to an old run-down chair and helped him sit down. Charlie turned on the television.

"I'll look for it Ben, you just sit here and watch T V till I find it." Charlie walked out of the room and carefully closed the door. He walked down the hallway and was met by his favorite nurse. Charlie just called her nurse Smitty, he never knew her first name

"Charlie, I asked the kitchen to make you a snack for today, you might get hungry before you come back." Smitty handed Charlie a paper sack with some sandwiches.

Charlie thanked her and continued down the hall to the outside door.
One of the nurses turned to Smitty and said, "That is the sweetest man in
this building, and you know he ain't got any family at all to visit him and
at his age he still wants to go to work."

"How old you think he is" asked the nurse.

"I don't rightly know, but he has to be over eighty," said Smitty.

"I bet he was a go getter in his younger days," said the other woman.

Charlie walked down the narrow sidewalk leading from the nursing home to the park across the street. He called it his short cut to work, but it was just a beautiful walk and he enjoyed it. He sometimes rested on a park bench and watched the birds play. Today he didn't feel like resting or even thinking about the good things in life. He was sick of living the lonely life that was now given to him. After both his sons were killed in the war he and his wife drifted apart and they didn't have much of a life. He wished he could go back and show her another side of himself. No matter how hard he tried that could never happen.

When she passed away there was no way he could keep their home. It was getting harder and harder for him to even walk down the drive way and get the mail. He wished several times he had built on a level lot and not one with an uphill walk and drive way. Betty had warned him about building on the hill but as usual he didn't pay any attention to her. After his wife passed away he sold out and came to this nursing home.

Charlie looked at his watch and tried to hurry his steps, but it seemed like he only had one speed and he was doing it now. The one story building had a reception area with a full time guard.

Why, Charlie never could figure out. The building held three attorney offices and they were not very respected in the small community. From what Charlie heard they were a little shady, but sometimes people need men like that to get them out of trouble.

"Morning Charlie," said the guard as the swinging doors slid on their circle entrance.

"Howdy Pete," answered Charlie. "Another day in paradise, right?"

"If you say so, Charlie. I don't see how you can always be in such a good mood."

"Just another day in the life of an old man," said Charlie as he smiled and walked on by.

If Pete only knew how Charlie felt on the inside he wouldn't think he was in such a good mood. Charlie was good at hiding his feelings. He made his way to the janitor's room off the main hall. He put his sandwich on one of the shelves and started arranging his cleaning chemicals and equipment.

Charlies first job was the conference room located between two offices. He figured the attorneys shared the room. It never was very dirty but

Charlie went through the motions of dusting and running the vacuum cleaner over the carpet. One of the side doors was open and Charlie walked over to shut it. Voices were coming from the next room.

"We knocked a home run yesterday, partner. That little trick you pulled on the judge left 'em reeling."

"You know I could get disbarred for that little trick, don't you?"

"Yeah, I know, but it helped us win the case and our part is a lot of money. In fact, it's so much we could pay our overhead for a couple of years and not work a day."

One of the men noticed the door to the other room was ajar and hurriedly went to shut it. He spotted Charlie on the other side. "You better get to work old man, we're not paying you to listen to us, you wouldn't know what we're talking about anyway. Now get back to work." The man slammed the door shut.

"Such greed," whispered Charlie. That's the only thing some people think about. Someday they will all be like me and then what good is all their money. If I did have a lot of money what would I do with it. Can't travel very far away from my doctor, seems like I need him more and more now. Can't buy any of those fancy cars, can't see good enough to drive one. Way too old to chase girls. Wouldn't do that anyway, I'm still true to Betty although she's been gone for three years.

He started the vacuum cleaner and remembered what his wife used to tell him. 'Keep your life free from love of money, and be content with what you have, for the man upstairs will always take care of you.'

That may be true, thought Charlie, but somehow, he felt over looked by the man upstairs. His life was just missing something and he could not put his finger on it. He used to ride motorcycles but his legs got so weak he had to give that up. Whatever his problem was he had to shake it. Charlie did not want to go on like this anymore. He finished cleaning the room and paused before leaving, looked around the room like someone was watching him and walked back to the door the attorney shut in his face. "Wonder what else they're talking about," whispered Charlie as he sat down on his water bucket and placed his ear on the door.

CHAPTER TWO

Charlie was listening with his ear to the door. It was against his better judgement and felt like he was doing something wrong, but for some reason he was pulled to the door to listen. The attorneys were getting louder and louder, like they were drinking and partying. It sure is early in the morning for them to start getting drunk, thought Charlie. But the way people live in this day and time he wouldn't put it past them.

The sound of voices grew louder and louder and drifted through the closed door.

One of the Attorneys started laughing as he spoke. "Can you believe what that old man Hightower wrote in his will. I couldn't bring that up or I'd been laughed out of the court room."

The other Attorney chimed in.

"There was no one left to mention it, every one of his family is long gone. We're the executors of his will so we can do whatever we want."

"Do you really believe there's anything to that story about a map and a mysterious find out in the desert his father told him about when he was a kid. The records show he talked about it some to his
children."

"Hell, yes I believed it. Where do you think all the money came from for the old man to start drilling for oil? Remember he started out with nothing but a dream and built it into one of the largest oil fields in the
country."

"Did you ever bring it up to the old man and ask him about it when he was alive?"

"Yeah, I did one time and he said he was making so much money now he didn't have time to make any more, and started laughing. I dropped it and never brought it up again. He said it was in such a rough part of the desert he didn't want to go back ever again."

"Did he even tell you what he found out there in the desert?"

"No, he never said what it was he found, only it was worth a lot of money and he used it to get started in the oil business."

"Sounds like a mysterious gold find to me. I've heard they were a lot of them in old days."

"Could be, but he never told me what it was."

Charlie heard the attorney stomp across the room and open a desk drawer. "Here's the old map he left me years ago. Want to go on a wild goose chase, or stay here and make more money?"

"I wouldn't venture out past the Holiday Inn, but I do wonder what he found out there in the desert?"

Charlie heard more laughter as he repositioned himself on the bucket. His eyes were as big as saucers. It was the first time Charlies heart beat this fast in a long time. Probably not since that time a boy with a new Harley parked in front of the nursing home to visit someone. Charlie walked out and just stood there in amazement on how beautiful a machine could be. His heart beat as fast then as it is now.

Charlie didn't move for an instant as he thought about what he had overheard. Is there a real map in there with directions to a lost gold mine? Could it be true about old man Hightower finding something in the desert that got him started in the oil business. Everyone in town knew he was loaded with money but never questioned how he got his start.

There was some more small talk between the attorneys about how they had pulled a fast one on the judge and got away with several thousands of dollars. The conversation made Charlie feel sorry for both of them. With their talent and money, they could do so much for this little town but instead they were focused only on how to make more money.

One of the attorneys told the other he had to run because of a hot date tonight. The other laughed at him and said. "Hope your wife never finds out, I'd need another partner."

"Hold on, I'll walk out with you."

Charlie hears the door to their office slam and then nothing but silence. He waited for a minute before getting off the bucket. His mind was cloudy and he acted a little confused. He started talking to himself.

"If there's a map in there that will lead someone to a lot of money it needs to be used by someone that will share it with the people around him. Who does the map really belong to? If I took the map would I be stealing. Never stole anything in my life. I don't know what to do."

Charlie started back to cleaning the room, but kept thinking about that map in the other room. Finally, he walked over to the door leading to the attorney's office and used his key to open it. Very carefully he stepped inside, like he was walking on eggs. In his mind he knew he was doing wrong but, in his heart, he felt like he was doing the right thing. He walked to the desk and slowly opened the big drawer. There in front of the all the papers laid a map. He reached for it like he was reaching for something hot. Carefully he pulled it out from the drawer.

"I can't just take it, they will miss it and wonder who took it," whispered Charlie.

He spotted a copying machine in the corner of the room and had an idea. I'll just copy the map and then no one will know I took it. He walked to the machine and studied it for a while, trying to figure out to make it work. The green light was on and he figured that meant it was ready to use. Very attentively he placed the map on the copying machine and pushed the button. A whiling noise startled him and he jumped back, thinking it might bring someone in the room to check on the nose. It suddenly stopped and a perfect copy of the map slid out the side. Charlie placed the original map back in the desk drawer and folded the copy and jammed it into his shirt pocket. He wiped his brow with his sleeve and breathed deep as he walked out of the room.

The rest of night shift was a blur as Charlies mind drifted back to the conversation between the attorneys. They didn't know what was out there in the desert only it was something that helped Hightower get started in the oil business. Whatever it is it had to be worth a lot of money, what could it be? When the shift was over Charlie couldn't wait to get back to his room and study the map.

CHAPTER THREE

For once Charlie had something to look at except his television set. People don't know how lonely a person could get with nothing but a television to keep them company at night. His room was rather quiet compared to some of the other rooms. His was on a hall where most to the residents were bed ridden and didn't get out much. He had purchased some small rugs to make the cold concrete floor a little more pleasant. God, he hated to walk on the cold floor barefoot when he first got up. He sometimes missed the feel of the thick carpet in his old home and the sweet smell of his wife lying next to him. These were just a few of the memories he had to get out of his mind, they did not do him any good, only to make him feel more and more lonely.

Charlie placed the map on his bed and rested on his knees studying it with great interest. Being an old truck driver Charlie had traveled up and down most of the highways in the area. The part that looked interesting and had several marks on it was in an isolated part of the county. Charlie had driven by that part of the state several times and never given it a second thought. No one wanted to go out there. Nothing but rabbit holes and rattle snakes. The oil companies didn't even bother to do any drilling in the area because it had already been checked on and everything showed negative for oil recovery.

The excitement was growing in Charlies mind. He had something to dream about, to think about, to talk about. Who could he share it with? Times like this is so hard on Charlie because he used to share everything with his wife and now there is no one to share it with. Charlies mind was ablaze with a young man's visions of adventures and excitement. He finally rested his head on the bed and slipped back to reality. He's in a nursing home with hardly no money and not one person to share his idea with.

Charlie suddenly raised up from the bed, a smile slowly grew on his face. He remembered his old friend Chester Marble. He hadn't seen him in years, but he would always listen to Charlies ideas and always give him some good comments. The last time he had heard about Chester he was living with one of his daughters across town. Hear she had fixed him up with his own room with a television and a phone. Charlie just had to talk to him about this map. How would he get there was the next problem? Something like this is too important to talk about over the phone.

Charlie sprung up from the bed and went to a cabinet under his television. He fumbled around in the back of it and pulled out a book on gardening. He opened the cover and there was a cut out hole in the middle of the book. In the hole was some folding money Charlie had been saving. Should I spend it on going to see Chestier or just sit on it for a rainy day?

"Charlie, what are you doing down

there on your hands and knees?"

A voice from behind him said. Charlie stood up and tucked the book under his arm. It was nurse Smitty, one of the nurses that Charlie liked.

"Thought I'd check on you sugar. Your kind of quiet today. Everyone in the hall wants to know if you're all right?"

"I'm just fine. Doing a lot of thinking and wanted to be alone for a while. While you're in here can I ask you to do me a favor? Will you look up a name for me in the phone book and write it down."

"Sure, Charlie, what's the name?"

"Chester Marble, is the name. And while you're at the phone will you please ask them how much a taxi ride from here to where ever you find is Chester's address?"

Nurse Smitty hesitated for an instant before answering. "Sure, I will Charlie. Is this Chester an old friend of yours?"

"He sure is. Haven't seen him in a few years. He lives with one of his daughters on the other side of town. We traveled many a mile on our Harley motorcycles. He was like a brother to me.

We kind of drifted apart when we got old and couldn't ride anymore."

The nurse knew that Charlie never had any

visitors and down deep she always felt sorry for Charlie. He lived such a lonely life. The word around the home is he had no family left, only memories. She had peeked in several times and caught him going through pictures in one of his scrap books he kept under the television. She thought she saw a tear one time when she walked in and found him looking at the book. He quickly closed it and smiled at her with that happy go lucky smile.

"Tell you what, Charlie. Why don't I take you to see Chester when my shift changes and you ride a taxi back? That way it'll save you some money. That sound good to you?"

Charlie grinned and shook his head in approval. "When can we leave?" asked Charlie.

"I've got a few things to take care of first and then we can leave. Say about thirty minutes," answered nurse Smitty.

"I'll be ready," said Charlie.

When the nurse walked out Charlie

was thinking what he would tell Chester. Should he tell him how he got the map? That would be admitting he stole something. Chester might not like that. Is Chester fit to go on an expedition like this? How we going to go? Neither of us have a car. A car would not do it, we would need a jeep with four-wheel drive. Maybe Chester and I can figure it all out. We used to solve problems with our Harleys when we would break down on the highways somewhere in the middle of nowhere. Boy, those were the days. Riding all day and night and so tired you couldn't

hardly walk and coming home to Betty who always had a good meal prepared for him. Chester's wife always did the same thing for him. They would brag the next day when they would meet for coffee on who had the best meal.

Charlie started giggling on what he was thinking. The last time he had anything to do with Chester was just before Chester's wife passed away. Charlies wife had been deceased for a year and Charlie was longing for some adventure. He still owned his home and the upkeep was getting the best of him. He just had to get away for a while. He persuaded Chester to go on a three day ride down into Mexico, which Chester didn't want to do. Charlie kept hounding him until he agreed to the ride. Against Chester's wife better judgement, they hit the road on their Harleys. The second day Charlie took some kind of stomach virus and had to be hospitalized for a week. The worse part it was in Mexico and Chester would not leave Charlies side. It was the worse week Chester had ever spent and he never did let Charlie live that one down.

Charlie folded up the map and put it in his shirt pocket and took a seat on the side of his bed. This is as good as any place in this room to wait for the nurse. He looked around the room and took a deep breath and released it. What kind of life is this, thought Charlie. A television sitting on a wooden cabinet, a wore out imitation leather chair in one corner and few shirts and an extra pair of pants in a small closet. What happened to all the beautiful things he and Betty accumulated in all the years of their marriage. Where had it all gone?

   Nurse Smitty knocked on the door. "Ready, sugar?"

CHAPTER FOUR

The drive only took a few minutes and Charlie wished it had taken longer. He couldn't remember how long it had been since he was allowed to sit back and enjoy the beautiful sights of the trees and beautiful lawns that outlined the street of their small town. The large cottonwood trees almost over lapped the street. He remembered how much pride he took in taking care of his own yard when he and Betty had their home. He hated it at the time but now wished he could work in his yard again. There was nothing but concrete around his nursing home and the small part where grass grew a yard boy was hired to keep it pretty. Charlie was deep in thought as nurse Smitty pulling in a drive way of a large brick home and stopped.

"This is the address, Charlie. Is that

your friend sitting on the porch?"

An old man was rocking in a wooden rocking chair dressed in a T shirt and a pair of well worn Jeans. He appeared to be taking a nap as Charlie opened the car door and started across the yard toward him.

"Make sure that's the right person, Charlie. Don't want to leave you out here by yourself," said the nurse.

Charlie stood in the yard for an instant and studied the old man in the rocking chair. He finally turned to the nurse. "That's him. Recognize him anywhere. We spent way too much time together years ago riding up and down these highways on our Harleys. I know that's him."

"Very well Charlie. You have a good time and I'll see you tomorrow."

The nurse drove away and Charlie approached the porch as a large smile slowly appeared on his face. He stepped on the stairs leading up to the porch he called out as loud as he could. "You old codger, wake up and smell the coffee."

The man in the rocking chair opened his eyes and turned his head in

Charlies direction. He was confused for an instant and finally started laughing. "You old rascal you. What in the world you doing over here? I didn't think they'd let you out of that home you live in." Chester stood up from his chair, a little slower than he wanted to, and walked over to meet Charlie and hugged his neck. There was an extra chair next to Chester's and Charlie sat down, a little exhausted from all the excitement.

"What brings you out here, Charlie? It's been a few years since we talked, you doing all right?"

"I'm in pretty good shape for the shape I'm in. Getting a little lonely sometimes, but I guess that's what growing old means."

Chester very slowly stood up and walked to a garden cabinet on the side of the porch. He pulled out some tools and finally started laughing as he removed a small bottle of Jack Daniels whiskey. "Been saving this for a rainy day, Charlie. Let's bust it open and live again, just like we used to do. Both men took very light pulls on the bottle, made faces like it tasted bad, and settled back in their chairs.

"Yeah, know what you mean, Charlie. All I got to look forward to is rocking on this porch and waiting till my daughter comes home and cooks me something to eat. Sometimes she takes me for a ride on weekends. That's about the story of how I live. Ain't too exciting. Not like we used to live when we rode our Harleys everywhere. Boy, those were the days. We were always getting in trouble."

Charlie put the bottle to his mouth and acted like he took another pull on the bottle but didn't drink anything. "The most exciting thing I've done is trying to convince the people at the nursing home to stop playing that God awful music on the intercom. I've told them time and time again to start playing some Elvis Presley, Chuck Berry, or maybe some Jerry Lee Lewis. Something to make us feel good again and not like we're going to a funeral."

"You having any luck convincing 'em, Charlie?"

"None what so ever."

to the mail box without getting tired. Both my knees are just about gone and all that cigar smoking I use to do has affected my breathing. How we gonna go up there in that rough county. We sure can't walk? I ain't got a truck with 4 wheel drive and I know you ain't."

Charlie hesitated for a moment before answering. "I have trouble putting on my underwear, much less walking, but I got this figured out, Chester. We take one of those four-wheel drive Jeeps. I've heard they'll go anywhere."

"Just where we going to get one of those Jeeps, wise guy?"

"I got an idea, Chester. Remember little Billy Tate that always wanted to go riding with us and we didn't let him 'cause he rode a Honda?"

"Yeah I remember him. Back then we thought we were king of the roads. Good little kid but we could not get him to ride a Harley. I remember one time he was mad at us and told us to take those Harleys and put 'em where the sun don't shine. He finally stopped coming around the shop. Don't remember what happen to him."

"I remember what happened to him, Chester.
He now owns Tate Motor Company. He grew up to
be a good business man who now owns a Jeep dealership. He's a big man in the car business. You should read the paper. If you do you'll see ads about him all the time."

"You mean the little boy we used to tease all the time is the same as the one who owns that Jeep dealership across town.?"

"That the same one Chester. He's all grown up now and probably made a lot of money."

"I know how you think Charlie Wise. You're thinking about asking him if we can barrow a Jeep. Don't know about that Charlie. We didn't treat him very good in the old days."

"Won't do any harm to ask him. Remember a blind squirrel can find an acorn every now and then and I think maybe we've found ours."

Chester slowly shook his head from side to side and started laughing.

"Charlie, this is why I enjoyed being around you in the old days. You always came up with some crazy idea. Some got us in trouble and some were exciting. Don't believe we can get in trouble on this one. I'm with you if Tate will let us have a Jeep. While you're at it why don't you ask him for some money for equipment too. Sleeping bags, food, maybe a tent. We don't have any idea of how long this will take. I ain't got any pressing business to attend to so let's act like it's a vacation."

Both old men shook hands and then hugged. "This might be our last one, Chester, so let's make it a good one."

CHAPTER FIVE

Chester had persuaded his daughter to drive them to the big Chrysler and Jeep dealership located across town. The men had counted their money and decided they had enough to ride a taxi back to Chester's place and then for Charlie to return to his nursing home. Chester's daughter didn't like the idea of them both going off together like this. She remembered some of the trouble her father and Charlie had gotten into and didn't want them to get into trouble again. She knew when Chester and Charlie got together it always spelled disorder. After some promising by both men she eventually gave her permission.

Charlie and Chester walked across the showroom floor and looked at the new shiny cars. No salesman offered to help them. Chester said it was because they looked like they had no money, which of course they didn't. Finally, a man walked up to them and asked if he could help.

In the most serious voice he could force out Charlie said. "We're here to see Mr. Tate on an important business matter."

"Is he expecting you, sir?"
"Don't think so, but I know he'll see us. Tell him his old riding buddies are here from years ago," said Charlie.

"And tell him we brought a Harley with us," added Chester.

Charlie and Chester both started laughing as the man turned and walked away. In a matter of minutes Billy Tate somberly walked up behind them with a scowl on his face. "Didn't think I'd ever see you two again. Looks like you've seen better days. What in the world can I do for you two old men? I know you can't buy a car so why you here?"

The cheerfulness attitude was now gone from Charlie and Chester. It was the same old Billy. They both now remembered why they didn't want him to ride with them. He was just no fun to be around.

"Billy, we just wanted to talk to you about a business deal," said Charlie. "I know we had some different views on things long ago but business is business." Charlie looked around the show room floor. "You didn't get all this by holding grudges now did you?"

A smile started to spread across Billy's face and then he started laughing. "You two old farts. I'll never forget you and the trouble you gave me about riding my Honda."

"We were only kidding you Billy," said Chester.

"Let's go back in my office and talk about the old days," said Billy as he turned and started walking toward his office.

Billy Tate's office showed how successful he had become in the town. The walls were decorated
with awards and trophies from helping the community with their drives of good will and his support of all the children activities. It was very obvious that Billy was an active member of the community. Billy walked behind a large desk and took

his high back chair. He motioned for Chester and Charlie to take a seat in front of his desk in an overstuffed leather couch.

"Now, what can I do for my old friends?" asked Billy.

Charlie and Chester looked at each other in a mindless fashion. Neither knew how to start the conversation. To get this far was Charlies idea and neither men knew what to say. Chester spoke first.

"Charlie has come across something we would like to do but we don't have the money. Let him tell you all about it and maybe you can furnish us with some transportation and a little equipment money."

Charlie told Billy the story about the map and how he came about it and the conversation he over head with the attorneys.

"Just who were the attorneys?" asked Billy.

Charlie hesitated before he told Billy their names.

"I know those two. Had several dealings with them both and don't care for either. Before we go into this any further do you have the map with you Charlie?"

Charlie pulled out the map from his shirt pocket and handed it to Billy. Charlie looked over at Chester like he didn't know if he should do this or not. Billy started studying the map and then started a little laugh.

"Do you guys know where this is? It's right in the middle of nothing. Not anything out there but an unoccupied area of waste." Billy placed the map on his desk and thought a while before saying anything. "Let me tell you two a story that has been circulated around town for many years. The rumor is old man Hightower found something out there that jump started his oil business. Whatever it was he took it to his grave. Now the real story is Hightower's grandfather and the man who used to own the land. They were partners. That land used to belong to an old cowboy named Washington. The old timers still call that part of the state Washington Ranch. Washington tried to raise cattle out there but the land was so rough he just gave up. That's where Hightower comes into the story. Old man Hightower's ancestor were pure bandits. He was pretty notorious in the last century. Anyway, he and Washington teamed up and stormed the country with robberies of everything from banks to trains."

Charlie and Chester were spell bound at the story and their eyes were wild with the energy of their youth. They both knew they were on the threshold of an adventure.

"There used to be Indians out in that part of state," continued Billy. "Washington and Hightower were continuously fighting them until the Indians just up and moved away. Same as the Mexicans who came across the border. Some people still say the two old men just killed anyone who came on the land. That's something we'll never know."

Chester asked in an excited voice. "What ever happened to the two men?"

Billy continued. "The way I heard it both got shot in a little village across the river in Mexico. They don't keep very good records of what happens down there so we have to believe in rumors."

"What happened to the ranch and the land?" asked Charlie.

"After several years the state took it back. He had some kids but they didn't have the money to pay the tax on the property. No one wanted the wasted land so it just sits there year after year. Several oil companies did some test drilling out there but they found nothing. Far as I know the land is full of snakes and ghosts of the past."

Billy stood up and walked to the coffee pot in his office. "You old adventurers want some coffee?" Billy then did a very strange thing. He shut the door to his office and walked back to his desk.

Charlie and Chester were still in shock by the story Billy told them. They finally cleared their head and answered. "We'd love some Billy."

"Help yourself boys."

Billy sat back down and studied the map some more. "Looks like the area is circled where something is located. Wonder what all the little Xs are in the circle?"

"Only way we gonna find out is go

up there and see for ourselves," said Charlie.

"Let me be straight with you two. I knew old Hightower really good. I was a pall bearer at his funeral. What I think he found up there in his old grandfather's land was some kind of gold mine. What he did find he invested to all in that first oil well and boy did he hit it big. I asked him several times what he found up there in the mountains. He never would say. Don't know if it was gold or something else."

Billy put the map down on his desk and started talking in a very serious tone. "Just what do you want from me, boys. I'm a pretty busy man and I sure can't go on a wild goose chase with you two."

"We ain't asking you to go with us, just asking for a loan of one of those Jeeps and maybe some equipment money."

Billy sat back in his overstuffed chair and thought for a moment. "Tell you what I'll do for you two. Why don't you sell me the map and forget about all this wild goose chase? You're both getting up there in years and I know that's rough

country. I really think you're be better off just selling me the map. It looks interesting and I can frame it and hang it on my wall. That
sound good to you?"

Charlie and Chester looked at each other like they didn't know what to say. It was the same old Tate, he wanted a part of everything and didn't want to work for it. "Don't know, Billy," said Charlie. "What do you think is a fair price?"

Chester jumped up from the couch and spoke in a demanding voice. "Now wait a minute, Charlie. You got me all primed up for another one of your adventures and now you going let me down?"

"Chester, we need to think about our health. By the way your daughter talked to me you need someone to help you every day. When we get out there in the desert ain't gonna be anyone to help you with anything. I ain't no nurse, Chester."

Billy thought a few seconds before saying anything. "Tell you what I'll do boys. After considering everything you two have told me I think I'll take some time off from this place. It'll be like old times, except this time I'll be leading on one of my Hondas and you two Harley boys will be dragging up the rear."

Cheater had a questionable look on his face. "What you mean me and Charlie be dragging up the rear?"

"Chester, I've got some Honda 4wheelers that make traveling in the desert a lot nicer. I lead the way because I know a little about that country and you and Charlie can follow me in your own 4wheelers. I'll supply everything that we need and go with you two old farts for half of whatever we find. Is that fair enough?" Billy folded up the map and handed it back to Charlie.

Charlie and Chester both shook their heads in approval. "When we gonna leave?" said Chester.

"Don't you guys worry about nothing, I'll handle everything. And Charlie, you take very good care of that map. We're in for an adventure."

CHAPTER SIX

Billy Tate drove the Jeep pulling the trailer with the 4wheelers. Chester sat in the front seat and talked about the old days of riding his motorcycle. Charlie stretched out in the back listening to the sound of the highway. The pulsation sound of the tires and the highway was like sweet music to Charlie. It brought back memories of the many times he and Betty traveled up and down this same highway on one of their weekend trips. She loved to travel. Charlie had really had enough being a truck driver but he knew Betty never got to go anywhere and he was always glad to take her on those overnighters. He had much rather stayed home but marriage is always fifty-fifty. That was the words Betty always used when they would get into an argument. He closed his eyes and, in his mind, could see her smiling when he would suggest a designated expedition for them. He wished she was with them now.

"Wake up back there, Charles," said Billy. He pulled off the road and drove on the shoulder for a while, looking for a turn off. There was no traffic on this part of the highway and in fact if someone broke down they would have to be out here a long time before any help would arrive.

"I think this is it boys," said Billy as he slowly drove to a wire fence gate. "Chester, you'll have to open it."

Chester opened the door of the Jeep and for the first time realized the loneliness of this part of the country. The heat hit him in the face and caused him to blink. Once you get used to air conditioning it's hard to face the desert so fast. Chester stood at the gate and listened. There was no sound at all. He felt a little faint but was not going to act like an old man and let Billy start laughing at him. He tugged at his pants and started strolling toward the gate like he was in good shape. When he pulled on the post he realized he didn't have the strength he used to and rested on the wire. Billy recognized the trouble Chester was having and jumped out of the Jeep to help him.

"Sometimes these gates are pretty hard to open, Chester. This one probably hasn't been opened in years."

Billy helped Chester open the gate and then went back to the Jeep and drove it through the cattle guard opening. Chester waited for Billy to pass through. A cloud of dust covered Chester as he tried to shut the gate. This time he overworked his muscles and managed to pull the gate close and proudly walked to the Jeep.

"I knew you could do it old man," said Charlie from the back seat.

The road apparently hadn't been traveled on in many years. In some ways it didn't look like a road, only an old worn path through the desert. With the Jeep there was no problem. The trailer was another matter. It seemed to bounce when they hit some of the sink holes in the road causing Billy to bring the Jeep to a crawl to be safe and not break anything.

"We don't want to lose our 4 wheelers and equipment," said Billy.

"When we asked you for help we had no idea you would equip us with 4 wheelers and all this camping gear. It's going to be like staying in a motel," said Charlie from the back seat.

"Don't be too sure of yourself," answered Billy. "This country is the worst you have ever seen. I was involved with an oil test drilling outfit up here a few years ago. We thought there might be some oil up here everyone has overlooked. No such luck. Every hole was dry. Wasted a lot of money on that little project."

The path became almost invisible and they were driving across nothing but wild desert and mesquite brush. The Jeep had gone as far as it could go and Billy pulled up beside a cluster of mesquite bushes. "This about does it for the Jeep. From now on it's going to be fun. Let's unload and set up camp and we can get an early start in the morning."

"Sounds good to me," said Charlie. They unloaded the 4 wheelers and the equipment and made camp just before the sun dipped behind the far-off mountains. The heat of the desert changed and with the last of the sun the temperature dropped fast. It wasn't long until Charlie had gathered some stumps of mesquite wood and set a blazing fire that chased away the night chill.

After a meal of beans and biscuits, which Billy probably had his wife prepare, Charlie and Chester started showing how tired they were. The glow of the fire danced off their faces telling Billy they both needed some rest.

Billy stood up from the fire and walked over to Charlie. "Before we all get some sleep let's look at that map again."

Charlie placed the map on the ground and used his flashlight so they could see better. Billy studied the map.

"By using the mountains for a location point I say we're about here," said Billy as he pointed to a place on the map. "We're not far from the Mexican border. Checked with some government people I know and they told me this area is so rough the Mexicans won't even try to cross over it. Several killings have also happened out here over the years which adds to the Mexicans fears of this land."

When Chestier heard Billy say killing he suddenly became more livelier. He moved over closer to Charlie. "What do you mean, killing? We ain't no mercenaries. We're just old men looking for something out here we don't even know what it is. What we gonna do if someone jumps on us. Dad gum it Charlie, what you got us into. Just like years ago you were always getting us in trouble."

Charlie stood up and placed his hand on   Chester's shoulder. "Settle down Chester. You wanted an adventure and that's what you're going to get."

Billy folded the map, handed it back to Charlie and turned to Chester. "I've been in places like this before, Chester. That's why I brought my pistol, and I know how to use it."

Silence fell over the camp as Chester darted his eyes from side to side. The fire light reached only a few feet out into the desert. The darkness sent a chill up Chester's back. He looked over at Charlie. "There better be something up here, Charlie Wise."

A sudden glow and bright light illuminated the distant sky. It was a long way off but intense brightness caused everything to glow for an instant. All men had concerned looks on their faces. Chester turned to Charlie with his mouth wide open but didn't say a word. "Ain't that the way we're going tomorrow?" said Chester in almost a whisper.

Billy tossed out what was left of his beans to the ground and said. "I believe it is Chester."

Chester and Charlie shared a tent while Billy had his own. Before drifting off to sleep Chester asked Charlie what he thought that bright light was that flashed in the sky.

"I've been thinking about that, Chester. Don't have any idea. Heard people talk about things like that but never seen anything like it and I've traveled up and down these highways many a mile."

It was deathly quiet for a moment and Chester spoke out in a whisper, like he didn't want anyone to hear him. "I've heard stories about things like this. Watched T V when they talked about

about unusual things happening out in the desert. Some of 'em makes my skin crawl too. I've decided it must be evil spirits looking for something. Maybe they're looking for the same thing we're looking for."

"Remember all those stores about cattle mutilations a few years ago? asked Chester. "You think we could be in the middle of all that?" Charlie hesitated for a moment before answering. "I thought that stopped years ago. They never did find out what caused it."

"I know what caused it Charlie, it was something not of this world. Had to be. That's why the government never would tell us what caused it. You know as well as me they never tell us the truth. Kind of wished I was back at my daughters' front porch about now. Maybe I'm too old for an adventure like this."

"You ain't too old for an adventure like this Chester. What's happened to you. There was a time when you would have charged out in the desert and ran right up to whatever it was and wanted to fight. Nothing would scare you. What's happened to you?"

"I'll tell you what's happened to me, Charlie Wise. I've gotten older and smarter than I use to be. That's what happened to me."

In the far distance a coyote cried out and Chester's eyes open wide and he turns to Charlie. "I don't think I like this place, Charlie."

CHAPTER SEVEN

The nights dampness quickly disappeared as the desert sun started its steady heat on the camp site. Chester slowly crawled out of his sleeping bag and tried to straighten up. He moaned and groaned and couldn't straighten up.

"What in the world is wrong with you Chester?" asked Charlie.

"I can't straighten up, Charlie. That ground is hard as a rock."

Billy was just coming out of his tent when noticed the trouble Chester was going through. He walked over to him and placed his boot on Chester's butt. He then grabs his shoulder and pulled back. Chester yelled out in pain.

"You'll get used to it Chester. Sleeping on the ground is hard to do until you get used to it. It just takes time," said

Billy.

It wasn't long until Billy had a good fire going and a pot of coffee brewing. "The way I see it Charlie we got to head up that way, toward the mountains. You make the map out that way too?"

Charlie moved where he could see the map that Billy had spread out on the sand. "Ain't no other way to go, Billy, except up that way toward the border. You ever been up that way?"

"Ain't many men gone up there, Charles. We'll be traveling in some never discovered land. It's going to be rough. Not much telling what we're gonna find up there." Billy stared up toward where they were going and took a deep breath. "Hope you guys can make it."

After they had some cold biscuits Billy poured what was left of the coffee on the fire and they prepared to travel. Billy pulled on his gloves and helmet and walked to the 4wheeler. Charlie did the same and looked over at Chester which had put his helmet on backwards. Charlie walked up to him and pulled it off and handed it back. "Put it on right, Chester. Have you forgot how to put a helmet on?"

"It's been a long time, cut me some slack."

Billy shouted out for them to follow him as the 4wheelers started up. Chester guns his and the front wheels come up and he fell off. He quickly jumped up and back on in hopes not one saw him. Charlie saw what happened and just shook his head in amazement.

The men traveled for the rest of the morning, dodging clumps of cacti, large rocks and drop-offs deep enough for the 4wheelers to get lost in. It was rougher than Chester or Charlie imagined and the day became so warm it was almost unbearable. They both thought the same thing. Maybe they didn't make the right decision on coming out in this forsaking land. About noon Billy held up his hand and parked under a mesquite bush where there was a sliver of shade. Charlie and Chester pulled in beside him.

Billy retrieved one of the containers from the back of his 4wheeler and sat it on the ground. He pulled out some water bottles and snacks and passed them around. The men rested with their own thoughts enjoying the break from the heat and listening to the quietness of the desert.

Chester all of a sudden shouted out. "I don't care how hot it is or how rough it is this is better than living the boring life I have. Don't think I'll ever go back to my daughters. I almost forgotten how it feels to be free."

"Now just where you think you're going to live, Chestier?" said Charlie.

"If we find something worth a lot of money I'm going to take my share and go to Mexico. Heard a man can live like a king for not too much money down there. And some of their doctors are just as good as we have here in the states." He looked over at Charlie and winked. "I ain't too old to chase those little Mexican girls either."

"Hate to break up your dreams but have you noticed those shiny lights up there in the mountains. I've been watching them for hours. Seems like they move from side to side. Very strange looking," said Charlie.

"I've been watching them too, Charlie," answered Billy;

All the men stared up into the distant mountains and didn't say a word. Charlie stepped off his machine and walked over to Billy. "Is there something you ain't told us Billy. Is there some other reason you wanted to join us on this adventure? You always were a little sneaky."

Billy rested on the seat of his 4wheeler as he drank his water. "Yeah, there is one thing I didn't tell you guys. Remember I told you I did some test drilling up here for oil?"

"I remember you telling us that," said Charlie.

"There something else I didn't tell boys about. I had a partner. He worked for the study of abnormal events. It's part of a government branch not many people know about. Before we started he told me a story. The reason no one comes up here is because of what the old timers around here think. Remember reading about all those cattle mutilations a few years ago?"

Charlie and Chester looked at each other and didn't know what to say. In a very timid voice Charlie answered. "Yeah,

I remember. The ranchers kept finding dead cattle with all their blood gone. Stopped as fast as it started. Everyone thought it was just some kids playing tricks."

"It wasn't any tricks, Charlie, this is where it all happened. The government couldn't explain it to the ranchers so it was kind of hushed up."

Chester threw down his bottle of water and stomped around saying some not so friendly words. He finally walked over to Charlie. "What in the world have you got us into this time?"

Billy tried to calm Chester down. "Now Chester, nothing's going to happen to you. It was only cattle that got mutilated. Never been a report of a man getting hurt. So, don't worry."

Chester kicked at the sand a few times trying to cool off. "Billy, you haven't changed a bit. You got an answer for everything. You ever thought that was why the Harley riders didn't like you, Mr. know it all."

Charlie walked over to Chestier and looked him in the eye. "Chester, that was a long time ago and everyone has changed. Billy is only trying to be honest with us."

"Just trying to make you feel more comfortable out here in this wildness, that's all Chester. If you remember there hasn't been a report of any cattle mutilations in years. So, don't you worry about it, everything is going to be OK." answered Billy.

"I guess you got an answer for all those bright lights we seen last night too," asked Chester.

"Well, as a matter of fact I do. There're all airplane lights from the military base at White Sands. Sometimes the planes get off course and the lights shine this way. Looks spooky but it's all perfectly normal. People been trying to make something out that for a long time. Ain't nothing to it, Chester."

Charlie broke the tension up and said. "According to the map we got a long way to go. Let's get moving." The three 4wheelers headed off toward a washed out ravine and soon were engulfed in the whirling sand of their machines. The land suddenly changed from the open desert to an unusual gathering of strange rock formations. Rocks seemed to have pushed themselves up from the desert floor. They were in all sizes, large and small. The drivers had to be careful not to run into one, it would have wrecked their 4wheelers.

After a few hours of hard riding Billy pulled over beside one of the large rocks. There was a small shade, just big enough for his machine, and he parked in it. Charlie and Chester parked their machines and walked over to the shade.

On top of one of the high ridges overlooking the desert where the boys had decided to rest an old Mexican man observed their every move. He was perfectly still, not moving a muscle, watching the three 4wheelers move further into the rugged part of this no mans land. He finally spit tobacco juice on the ground and moved away from the ridge.

"Let's look at that map again, Charlie," said Billy. Charlie laid the map on the sand in the shade and they all studied it. "From here it starts getting pretty rough. Don't know if we can make very good time. Don't think we can use our machines anymore. I know you two have a hard time walking but you got to from here on. Don't think it'll be far. I say we make camp here and start off early in the morning after you two get a good night's rest. That sound good to you guys?"

Charlie and Chester were exhausted and the sound of making camp sounded good their ears. It didn't take them long to have everything ready for a good night's rest. Chester hoped it would be better than the night before. Maybe Billy was right it just took a little getting used to.

After some more beans and biscuits the men retired to their tents. Darkness soon surrounded them and the camp fire gradually burned down to only a few bright chunks of hard mesquite wood which glowed in the dark.

Charlie squirmed in his sleeping bag trying to get comfortable. He felt a little blue because he was having such a good time and there was no Betty to share it with. He started to develop a soreness in his shoulders from the riding and wished Betty was here to rub his back. He pulled the sleeping bag up under his chin and tried to sleep but his every thought was about his deceased wife. How much longer would it take for him not to think about her every minute of the day.

"Charlie, you asleep yet?" asked Chester.

"Not yet, Chester. You doing all right, partner?"

"Wanted to ask you something. You feel something ain't right about all this?"

"Yeah, I sure do. Seems like Billy knows more about what we're after then we do. I knew he was a take control kind of guy, but I never knew he was this strong. I just feel like you do, something ain't right about this. He wanted to come with us for some reason. Business men like him don't take off from their lives for a wild goose chase."

Chester tosses in his sleeping bag and turned toward Charlie. "I bet he knows what we're after. He probably knew what was up here when we came to see him. Remember he told us he was a good friend of old man Hightower. He probably told him something about all this but he just didn't have a map. When you told him about the map he jumped into action. He's still like the old Billy Tate we used know. Never could trust him."

Charlie didn't say anything for a moment and then broke the silence of the desert night. "Now that I've been thinking about it I believe those shiny objects we kept seeing up on the mountain were following us."

Chester sat up in his bed roll. "Just what do you mean by someone following us?"

"Well, they moved like we did and stopped like we did. Just like someone was watching us. Don't know who it could be but I think it was human."

"Dang, you Charlie. This ain't no fun adventure like you promised me."

"Get some sleep, Chester, I got a feeling we're going to have a busy day tomorrow.

CHAPTER EIGHT

The first thing they did was hide the 4wheelers in a cluster of mesquite bush. Chester couldn't figure out why Billy wanted to hide them. "Ain't no good thinking person would be here, except us. Makes no since to me."

Billy told him if they can be seen sometimes people from across the river come over and steal what they can and those 4wheelers are worth a lot of money in Mexico. Chester thought about it for a while and then continued throwing brush on the machines. When they were finished Billy looked at their work and shook his head in agreement. They left on foot.

The traveling was at a dead crawl. Chester had a hard time breathing and the pain in Charlies knee gave him fits. The heat of the desert blazed down on the men. Billy had to stop several times just for Charlie and Chester to catch up with him. It seemed like he was possessed with what they were doing.

At one rest period Charlie tried to watch what he thought to be something following them up in the mountain. Whatever or whoever it was could look down on them with ease. Although it was a long way away they could be using binoculars and watch the groups every move.

The party came to a narrow ravine and looked for a way to cross. Chester suddenly lost his footing and rolled to the bottom. Charlie slid down the side of the ravine and the first to get to him.

You all right Chester?" What happened to you?"

Chester rolled over from being on his back and looked up at Charlie. "I fell, Charlie. Can't you see what happened. I think maybe I sprung something. My leg feels funny."

Billy worked his way down the ravine and dropped to one knee beside

Chester. "That was a bad fall, old man. You all right?"

"No, I ain't. I need to rest. This is not any fun."

Billy examined Chester's leg and determined it was just bruised and he would be fine. They decided it would be good time to make camp and let Chester rest before striking out again in the morning.

That night around the camp fire there was not much talk. The fun was gone on the so called adventure and Charlie and Chester both wanted some answers before going on any further.

Charlie poked the fire and brought the flames higher. They reflected off Billy's face as he sat by himself across from Chester and Charlie.

"We've followed you this far Billy without asking any questions and now we need to know just what me and Chester are getting into? I think you know more than you have told us. How about coming clean with us Billy?"

Billy sat frozen, he didn't move a muscle as he stared into the fire. Charlie and Chester were on the opposite side of the fire and watched Billy very close. Neither put much trust in him. Billy finally got to his feet and walked back and forth in front of the fire. "Yeah, there's a lot I didn't tell you boys. I didn't tell you because I thought you wouldn't believe me for one reason and the other is I wanted what we're looking for all for myself."

"Just what in the hell we looking for, Billy?" asked Charlie. "We both thought it might be gold, as did everyone in town. You act like it's not gold, so what in the hell we looking for?"

Billy reached in his shirt pocket and pulled out a cigar. Took his time lighting it and finally puffed on it some before answering. "The government knows what caused those cattle up here to be like there were, they just didn't tell the public. Whatever you think of me never under estimate the people I know and the information I can get hold of. This all comes from a very reliable source, so don't question it."

"Billy, you were always full of bull so don't tell me anything about flying saucers or anything like that," said Charlie.

"It ain't about flying saucers, but you're getting warmer. Remember those lights everyone talks about seeing up here? Well, old man Hightower wanted to find out and he came up here. He found out the lights were from experimental air planes the Government was testing over at White Sands. Sometimes the planes would get off course and swing over this part of the desert. When they do their lights are very bright and could be seen a long way from here and they would scare the hell out of everybody. That solved the problem of the lights but the most important thing he found was small pallets covering the ground after a plane came in low"

Charlie and Chester were spellbound and didn't say a word, they sat fascinated by Billy's story.

"These experimental air planes were all nuclear powered by stuff we don't know about yet. Some kind of experimental rocket powered engines. When they come over the mountains over there they emitted some kind of small pellets from their engines. Old man Hightower found out the rubbish the planes emit was a chemical residue called rhodium. It's very rare. Hightower found out about this and gathered some up. He sold it for a fortune. The rest is history."

"Now wait a minute, Billy. You tell us Hightower picked something off the ground that was worth a lot of money," asked Chester.

"That's right, Chester. The pellets were also eaten by the cattle. That's what happened to them and why the government would not tell anyone about what was happening to them."

"Just what is this stuff called rhodium used for? If it's so expensive why ain't we ever heard of it?" asked Charlie.

"Well, for one thing it's used by the car manufactures for exhaust systems and a lot of things I don't understand, mostly in the chemical world. At that time, it was used for some kind of power for those experimental engines on the air planes. And the experimental plane they were testing spit out some from their engines when they come in over this part of the desert."

"You saying we going to pick up some rock like things from the desert floor? What good is the map if everything is on the desert floor?" asked Chester.

"No, it's not on the desert floor anymore. The planes stopped using those experimental engines and they don't spit it out anymore. However, Hightower gathered up several boxes of it and buried it out here in the desert. That map is where it is. Only thing I can't figure out is all those X's. He told me he buried it all in one place. Can't figure out what he meant by circling all those X's. Can't thank you boys enough for bringing me the map. I tried for years to get Hightower to tell me where this place was. He just wouldn't do it."

Charlie and Chester were silent, completely quiet. Charlie poked the fire one last time and asked Chester if he needed any help getting to the tent. Both men acted like they didn't even hear what Billy told them. Neither made any comments. Chester shook his head and tried to stand. He carefully stumbled toward his tent and fell through the flap. Charlie followed. Billy stood by the fire smoking his cigar and softly snickered at the men as they stumbled to their tents.

Charlie and Chester laid perfectly still, not saying a word. They couldn't believe what they just heard. After hearing Billy make his way to his tent Chester whispered to Charlie. "Charlie, we've experienced some pretty wild goose chases but I don't believe we ever been on one like this."

Charlie let out a very quiet, "that's right Chester, we ain't never been on something like this."

Chester tossed in his sleeping bag. "How far your recon we are from the 4wheelers. It would be all right with me if we just started back tomorrow and let this crazy man find whatever he's looking for by himself."

"Let's wait one more day and see what happens. I got the map so we can find our way back anytime we want to. And another thing, have you noticed how he acts like he knows where he's going. He ain't asked to look at the map all day."

"I hate to say it Charlie but I ain't never going to go with you on another one of your adventures. If I ever get back to my daughters I'm going to stay there till my time comes. I ain't leaving."

"What about your idea of going to Mexico, you give up on that?"

"I ain't give up dreaming, and that's all it is. I'm too old for anything like that. Sometimes I think the world has just passed me by. I don't even know what rhodium is. Never heard of it.   Lord knows what else I'm missing out on by sitting on the porch at my daughters house and just letting the world go by."

Charlie thought about his nursing home and his little room and decided how ever hard this was it was better than staying in that little gray colored room. He knew his time was getting close and until then he was going to enjoy life. Betty told him the day she died to enjoy every day of his life and never stop his adventures. They would be together again someday, so don't worry about anything, enjoy your life. Charlie pulled his sleeping bag up under his chin and went to sleep.

CHAPTER NINE

The next day Charlie and Chester were very quiet as they drank their coffee around the morning camp fire. Billy acted a little uneasy too. The atmosphere was bleak.

"This don't change a thing," said Chester. "if it's worth more than gold what we crying about. I'll still have enough to go to Mexico when we find the stuff."

"When we find the stuff, you'll have more than enough to go to Mexico, Chester," said Billy as he poured the remainder of his coffee on the ground. "We need to get started. I believe the place we're looking for ain't to far from here."

The progress of the men was again at a crawl because of Chester's leg. It was painful and his limp became worse.

At one time Charlie had to help him over some sandy mounds and then across a narrow ravine.

"We need to get to this place pretty fast, Charlie. Don't know how much longer I can keep up this pace," said Chester.

They suddenly came to a drop off in the desert floor. It was a steep cliff with dug out stairs chiseled into the side of the hard dirt. They all stopped and studied the steps and noticed how rough the terrain looked below. It was different from then desert they had been traveling in for the last few days.

"We got to go down there boys, I think we're getting closer."

Billy acted excited and was the first to start down the carved-out steps. He was very careful and took his time. Chester was next with Charlie helping Chester by tying a rope around his waist. The going was slow but they finally made it to the bottom of the ravine. Charlie untied the rope and they started following Billy into the rugged floor of the strange chasm. Large rocks appeared like they were sticking up from the desert floor.

The boys couldn't walk in a straight line without running into one of the strange formations. Very little vegetation was on the floor which made the place look like nothing was alive. Chester turning to Charlie and said. "This place is dead."

In a short time, they came to a bend in the floor of the ravine and when they rounded it there was a lean-to built of poles and pieces of flapping worn out canvas. Old tools and equipment were laying on the ground in all directions. The boys cautious walked up to the remains of the lean-to. Billy started getting more excited and displayed more emotion than he had shown since they started this adventure.

"This is the place, boys," said Billy. "This is where old man Hightower told me about. He buried his find right here. He said it was at the entrance to an old mine. He told me there was an old lean-to in front of the mine. This has to be it."

Billy looked inside the lean-to and noticed metal pots, and cooking pans like someone had spent some time at this location. Chester noticed an old rusted knife, half buried in the sand, and very carefully made his way toward it. He waited until no one was watching and picked it up and tucked it in his pants.

"What's the old mine for? Reckon it's an old gold mine?" asked Chester.

"Ain't nothing in there," said Billy. "Hightower told me it worked out years ago."

Chester thought for a moment and said. "There might be something left. We need to check it out."

Billy ignored him and walked over to Charlie. "Let's see the map again and get our bearings."

Charlie handed the map to Billy and said with a serious voice. "Need to ask you something. If someone wanted to hide something here why didn't they just put it in the old mine. Seems like a lot of trouble to bury out here when he could have just stored it in the mine."

"Don't ask me how the old timers thought. Maybe it was because like Chester said. If someone came out here the first thing they would do is check out the mine and they would find what he hid." Billy unfolded the map, dropped to his hands and knees and straightened it out on the ground. Billy joined him and they both studied the map.

"Still can't figure out what these X's mean. There're all over the place. Don't know where to start digging."

Chester was holding himself up, using an old stump, not putting much weight on his bad leg. He noticed Billy's shirt was pulled up in the back and a holster with a gun attached to his belt. He never noticed it before and wondered why Billy was now wearing it. Chester felt for the knife he hid in his pants and wrapped his hand around the handle. He had a bad feeling about this complete adventure but couldn't put his finger on just what it was. Billy suddenly stood up and started ordering Chester and Charlie on what to do.

"Chester, you start digging by that stump you're resting on. Charlie, you start digging over there by the entrance to the old mine."

"Just what we going dig with, our hands?" asked Charlie.

Billy reached in his back pack and pulled out two folding shovels. He tossed one to Charlie and one to Chester. "Now start digging. This is what you wanted now here it is, start digging." Billy attitude changed almost immediately when they found the mine site. He acted like a man who became possessed or in another world. His eyes were glassed over and he moved almost in double time. Charlie had a serious look on his face as he looked over at Chestier and slowly shook his head from side to side. They had ridden their Harleys so long together they almost could communicate without speaking. Chester nodded. They were into something they didn't know how to get out of. Several times in their motorcycle riding days they stumbled into situations where they wished they had not been involved and somehow managed to work their way out. One time Charlie mouthed off to a gang of Mexican bikers and they surrounded Charlie and Chester with their knifes drawn. There would have been a terrible fight if Chester hadn't stepped in and apologized for Charlie.

With Charlie and Chester's weak strength the digging was slow. Billy watched them and every now and then he would walk around in a circle kicking at the ground, and mumbling to himself.

"We got a real crazy here, Charlie," said Chester.

Billy heard Chester and shouted at him, "You two will do like I say. It ain't like the old days where you told me what to do. It's my turn now."

Charlie threw down his shovel. "You're just like the attorneys I clean for. You've got a good business, probable all the money you need, and you want more. I don't understand people like you. Chester and I trusted you and it looks like you're just like you used to be, no good."

Charlie stood staring at Billy for a moment and then picked up his shovel and started digging. He whispered to Chester. "You think you could find your way back to the 4 wheelers?" asked Charlie.

"Don't know if I can even make it back, Charlie. My legs are about gone. Fraid' my age is catching up with me old friend. If we get out of this mess it's going to have to be all yours, sorry."

Charlie didn't know how but he was going to get them out of this mess. He

He got 'em into it and he would get 'em out.

They dug the rest of the day with Billy watching them and telling 'em where to dig. They didn't find anything in any holes. Billy would laugh to himself and sometimes whisper things like, "I knew I would get even with these two for all the heart aches they caused me in my youth."

When night came Billy dug into his pack and came out with some beef jerky and handed it to the boys. "You two sleep in the old ran down lean-to and rest up because tomorrow you're going to be digging all day. Whatever Hightower buried has to be here."

As the sun descended on the far side of the ravine it became dark very fast. With the darkness also came the chill of the desert night. Charlie and Chestier were restless in their sleeping bags as they planned their escape. Chester told Charlie he had a knife he found in the sand if they need it.

The ground suddenly started shaking and a terrible roar almost deafened the men. Charlie immediately jumped out of the lean-to. He was met by a light so bright he had to cover his eyes. Billy was already outside and laughing. Billy looked over at Charlie and said, "This is one of those airplanes I told you about. It's coming in low. The lights are what everyone sees and thinks it's some kind of spaceship. We're on the right track, Charlie. We're going to find where Hightower buried his stash and make a lot of money."

Chester crawled out of the tent as the lights disappeared over the mountains and the thundering roar stopped. Once again, the silence of the desert surrounded them.

"What in the Sam Hill was that?" asked Chester. He sounded a little shaken by the sound of his voice.

Charlie turned to him and answered. "That my friend was one of the airplanes Billy told us about. He might be telling us the truth after all, Chester."

Billy shouted back at them. "Dang right I'm telling you the truth.

Now go back to sleep, we got a busy day tomorrow."

CHAPTER TEN

After a breakfast of more beef jerky and coffee Billy prodded the boys to start digging again. The area where Billy wanted them to dig was the sector in front of the mine entrance. According to the map that was where all the X's were marked and buried rhodium should be located. After a day and half of digging nothing had been uncovered. Billy was fit to be tied. His temper was getting the best of him and he cursed everything Charlie and Chester did. Nothing was right. He thought Charlie and Chester planned this and had already taken the rhodium before now and tricked him. He started to get crazier and crazier by the hour. Something had to be done.

Charlie walked over to Billy and very calmly says to him. "Billy, I don't think there's anything up here. I noticed a lower part of the ravine that could have been the place Hightower meant when he drew the map. I could go down there and give it a try if you want." Charlie knew how to talk to people when they got in the frame of mind like Billy. He'd seen the nurses talk like this many time at the nursing home to an older person when they became frantic and had to be calmed down.

Billy walked over to the edge of drop off and studied the ground below. He looked at the map again and started shaking his head like he agreed with Charlie. Charlie looked over at Chester and winked. Chester knew what Charlie had in mind.

The drop off was a slippery sandy patch of desert that would make a perfect slide. There were no rocks or any vegetation, only sand. Charlie held his shovel in hand and slid down the incline. In his mind he could see the map and a light bulb went off in his head. This could be the place the map really shows us. He didn't say anything as he planned his move. There was one large rock at the edge of the ravine which Charlie would imagine as entrance to the old mine. But he needed the map to see about all the little Xs that were drawn. As he looked around he noticed small piles of rocks stacked up in different locations. They were covered with sand but still he could make out they were put there on purpose. Charlie noticed one pile of rocks a little larger than the rest. He slowly walked over to it and moved the stack with his foot so no one could see where it had been.

"I think I might have found something down here," shouted Charlie.

Billy hurriedly pulled a small metal box out of his pack and almost fell down the incline getting to Charlie. "What have you found?" Billy dusted himself off after he stood up from sliding down the side of the ravine.

"There's some strange markings down here. I think they could match the map where the X's are located." Billy grabbed the shovel from Charlies hand and rapidly started digging where one of the rock piles was discovered. Chester had made his way over to the side of the ravine and looked over with amazement. He knew Billy was not the man he used to be and something had to be done to control him. Chester observed Billy as he tossed sand over his shoulder like a mad man. Suddenly Billy started yelling, screaming and laughing at the same time. "This is it boys. This is where Hightower hid his stash. Come and look."

Charlie walked over to where Billy stood trashing the sand and noticed a small silver colored box he had uncovered. He started to reach for it and Billy hit his arm with the shovel. "I wouldn't do that if I was you Charlie. It might still be active."

Charlie pulled his hand back and looked up at Billy. "What do you mean active? How we going to carry it back to the truck if it's active, as you say?"

"There ain't much in there Charlie and we going to transfer it to my lead thermos bottle I been carrying. Why you think I've been toting this heavy thing with me?"

Billy almost flew up the side of the ravine as he went to his pack and pulled out a thermos bottle and a pair of strange looking gloves. He almost fell down the slope getting to the spot where Charlie had found the silver package. Billy held the metal box he had retrieved from his pack over the container and it started making an electric beeping sound just like a metal detector. Billy was ecstatic as he placed the metal box on the sand it kept emitting an electrical sound. He smiled from ear to ear as he started laughing. He hurriedly placed his gloves on and opened the package. To Charlie it looked like a cluster of small rocks. He cautiously poured the contents into the thermos bottle and closed the top. He then did a strange thing, he tossed the bottle to Charlie who caught it.

"See how heavy that is Charlie. You noticed it wasn't even half full. I'd say we had about a pound. At five thousand dollars an ounce you're holding maybe a few thousand dollars' worth. There's a lot more out here, Charlie, and we're gonna find it."

The rest of the day was spent by Billy watching Charlie dig in all the marked spots. Every place Charlie dug there was nothing to find. Charlie never went to the place where he moved all the rocks and he tried to avoid that location the best he could.

Late that afternoon Charlie looked up at the sky and noticed large clouds forming in the West. "The suns fixing to go behind those clouds, Billy, and it's gonna get dark pretty fast tonight. How about us stopping until tomorrow? I don't think anything's gonna run off from us. Maybe tomorrow Chester's leg will be better and he can help us."

Chester's leg was getting worse as he watched from above. He couldn't hardly walk. He did manage to have a fire going when Charlie and Billy made their way up the ravine to the camp.

There was not much to eat and Chester was getting weaker and weaker. Not only from his leg but from no food. He always complained to Charlie if he didn't eat he couldn't think straight and would start to get dizzy. Of course, Charlie would always laugh at him but they did stop more than the other riders when they were on the road.

The dark clouds rolled up on them and a sudden flash of lightening startled the men. The lean-to didn't have much of a roof and it would not be a very dry place to spend the night. The rain started lightly and then became a flood as water poured on the men. They all had the same idea at the same time. They ran to the old mine shaft. It had caved in years ago but there were a few feet protected from the weather and the men huddled against the dirt wall. Not much was said as Chester's stomach started growling.

"I told ya Charlie if I don't eat I get weak. I can't hardly stand up now."

Billy heard him and snickered. "If you want any of this money we gonna get from selling this stuff you got to work for it old man. Just like me and Charlie. Tomorrow we all go digging."

Billy pulled up his sleeping bag which he had managed to bring into the mine with him and leaned up against the wall like he had no problems. In a matter of minutes Billy was sound asleep.

Charlie whispered to Chester. "Tomorrow we make our move."

Chester handed Charlie the old rusted knife he had found. "This might come in handy. Hope you don't have to use it, but you never can tell when you're dealing with someone like Billy."

A close lightening flash rumbled in the sky and the sudden glare on Charlie and Chester's face showed their age and the exhaustion in their eyes.

The rain stopped and the night chill covered the men in the cave. With no fire the sleeping was difficult. In the distance a lone coyote could be heard among the sounds of the insects buzzing around the necks of the men in the cave. A solitary man walked through the darkness toward the entrance of the cave. He stopped and studied the men wrapped in their sleeping bags. He was mean and dirty looking with bandoliers filled with bullets around his neck. Two large pistols were on his hips. He spit tobacco on the ground and turned and disappeared into the darkness.

CHAPTER ELEVEN

When Charlie and Chester woke from their cramped position in the entrance of the cave Billy was nowhere to be seen. Charlie walked over to the side of the ravine and noticed Billy already down where they had first found the box of rhodium. He had found a piece of screen and was tossing sand through it. Some strange looking pieces were not going through the screen. He wore his gloves and his metal box rested beside the pile of shifted sand that did not go through the screen.

Charlie walked back to Chester. "This is our chance to get this over with. I'm going down there and help him do what he's doing and when we start coming up the side of the ravine I want you to hall back and hit him as hard as you can with that piece of wood." Charlie pointed to an old fence post laying in the sand. "He should fall backwards and roll down the side of the ravine. Leave the rest to me. Can you do that, Chester?"

Chester took a deep breath and pulled up his pants. He was having a hard time standing with his hurt leg. "You mean like the time I hit that guy with a baseball bat when he chased you around the motorcycles?"

"Yeah, like that time. But don't fall over your motorcycle like you did then."

"There ain't no motorcycles to fall over out here. Wish there were and we could just ride away from all this mess you got us into."

Charlie didn't stay a word as he turned and started down the ravine toward Billy. He noticed Billy now kept his pistol in plain view, like he wanted to let them know he was armed.

"Find any more of that radioactive stuff down here, Billy? How much you going to try to get before we head back home?"

"I ain't leaving until we get it all," said Billy.

"Just how do you know you got it all? You don't know how many boxes he buried up here," answered Charlie.

"That's where you're wrong, my old fiend. There's something I didn't tell you and Chester. My mother was a cousin to old man Washington, the partner of Hightower's when they were outlaws. Remember he owned this land at one time. It was a family secret that not too many people knew about. My mother told me years ago about a place up here with enough treasure to last a man the rest of his life. I think we only found what Hightower buried. But according to my mother there's treasure up here from the old days when Hightower's grandfather and Washington were bandits. So, we're staying until we find the mother lode."

Charlie looked over to where he had moved the rocks. That must have been where something was hidden a long time ago. "How come you never did try to find this place until we came along? Was it the map?"

"Yeah, partly. I had an idea of where it was located but as you can see this place is a bad place to explore, it all looks alike. Mother would always make me promise her not to come up here. She thought there was still Mexican outlaws from across that border that would come over here. When she passed I got so busy with my dealership I just didn't have time to explore"

"Is that why you brought that gun in your pants?" asked Charlie.

Billy stood up from his throwing sand through the screen and walked toward Charlie. His eyes were glazed with hatred. "I found out years ago that you and Chestier didn't like me and the feeling is the same here. I wanted something to even up the score if you two started to treat me like you did years ago. Remember how you always made me the last in line to anything we did. How you made me do all the clean up around the shop. You said if didn't I couldn't go on any rides with you. And then when I did get to go with you I would have to always ride in the back and you two would always try to run off and leave me. Things like that have never left my mind. It ain't going to happen again. That's why I have this gun."

Charlie wanted to say a lot to Billy about the old days but decided it would not do any good. Billy's mind was so filled with hate there was nothing Charlie could do to change it.

"Billy, let's go up and drink some coffee before we start to work. I'm sure Chester has some cooking over the fire by now. He had it going good before I came down here. I want you to look at his leg again. It may be getting better today and he can help."

Billy pulled off his gloves and started toward the side of the ravine. "For once I'm going to agree with you. I've been up since sunrise and haven't had my coffee yet. I noticed you were up sometime last night and walked around the camp site. What's your problem, couldn't sleep?"

"What makes you say that?" asked Charlie.

"There's foot prints all over the ground. The rain made the ground soft and they're everywhere. Just figured you couldn't sleep, that's all."

Charlie was confused with what Billy said but didn't act like it meant anything to him. His mind was busy on what he would do when Chester hit Billy when they were coming up the side of the ravine.

Charlies plan was for him to be the first up the side and be clear when Chester hit him. Billy had beat him to the side of the ravine and started making his way to the top. Charlie could see Chester waiting on wobbly legs and hoped he had enough strength to do some damage with the old log. When Billy was almost over the ridge Chester drew back and hit Billy in the chest with the fence post. Billy staggered back and pulled his pistol. As he fell backward he fired at Chester. Billy fell backward on top of Charlie and they both tumbled to the bottom. As they rolled Charlie tried to take the pistol from Billy but it was no use, he could not over power him. Billy suddenly let out a blood screaming yell as he and Charlie stopped tumbling. A large rock, half buried in the sand with a pointed edge had struck Billy in the leg as he rolled. The pistol he held in his hand went flying away from them. Charlie caught a glimpse of it and jumped toward where he thought it would end up. He was right. The pistol landed only a few feet away and he jumped toward it. Charlie grabbed the pistol with both hands, jumped up and pointed it toward Billy.

"The tables have turned now you no good son of a gun. We're getting out of here and heading home." Charlies expression changed as he studied Billy laying on his back in the sand. Billy was in pain. Charlie immediately knew what was wrong. A bone struck out of Billy's pant leg. He had broken his leg.

CHAPTER TWELVE

Chester shouted out from above. "What's going on down there? Charlie, you all right? I think Billy shot me, but it ain't bad."

Charlie looked up the ridge and yelled up to Chester. "We got a problem. Billy broke his leg. We got to get him some help as fast as we can. How bad you shot?"

Chester mumbled to himself. "I ain't gonna help that son of a gun" Chester almost fell down trying to look down the ravine. Blood was running down his side. Billy had shot Chester in the shoulder. It was not life treating, but painful. He held his arm and finally got in a position to study what was going on below. He didn't like what he was looking at. Charlie was bending over Billy's leg trying to apply a splint from a shovel handle. He could see blood had soaked the bandana Charlie used to tie it up tight. He jumped up as fast as he could and went to their back packs. For some reason he had brought a rope. Chester always packed things you would never need. This time it would come in handy.

"Charlie, I'm sending down a rope. Tie it under his arms and we're pull him up."

Charlie secured the rope under Billy's arm. "Pull it tight Chester, I'm coming up to help." As Charlie started to walk away Billy let out a groan. "What's happening to me? Charlie, you hear? My God Charlie, I'm hurt, really bad, need some help, don't you leave me."

Charlie went back to Billy and knelt down beside him. "Billy, you fell and broke your leg. I'm going to try to pull you up the ravine and then we'll try to get you some help. This might hurt, but grit your teeth. We got to get you up." Billy's eyes started to glaze over and he looked like he was going to pass out.

Charlie scampered up the ravine as fast as he could where Chester was trying to watch what was happening. He stood against a rotten fence post for help. Blood soaked the front of his shirt and was running down his arm. When Charlie reached the top, he rushed over to Chester and noticed what had happened to him.

"Billy's shot must have hit you. Let me look at it before we pull Billy up. "Charlie tore open Chester's shirt and found a wound in the front and back of the shoulder. The bullet went straight through and apparently didn't hit a bone. It looked like a clean wound. Charlie remembered a first aid kit he had seen in Billy's pack and went straight for it. He opened the kit and took out some ointment and put it on Chester's wounds. The blood stopped and Charlie used the tore up shirt of Chester's for a bandage. Chester hadn't said a word as Charlie worked on him.

"Does it hurt, Chester? You got any pain?"

Chester took a deep breath before answering. "I'm still a hundred and fifty pounds of blue twisted steel. A little bullet ain't going stop me." His eyes rolled back and he fell to the ground.

"I've got to pull Billy up," whispered Charlie. You get up from there and help me. "I'm in a mess here and I need your hundred fifty pounds of blue twisted steel,"

Chester moaned and slowly stood up on his good leg. "Guess I ain't as tough as I used to be. What we gonna do Charlie?"

"I got to pull him up Chester. His leg is broke and a bone is sticking out. If you can help me I really need it."

Chester had a surprised look in his face. "I've said some bad things about him, Charlie. I'll take 'em all back and help you as much as I can. But my leg is getting bad. I can't hardly stand up by myself and I got a bullet hole in my shoulder." He looked at Charlie with sad eyes. "Charlie, we're in a dangerous way. I'm hurt, Billy's hurt, we ain't got much water left and you're an old man. Don't know how you're going to do it my friend, but you got to get us out of here."

"I'll worry 'bout that when we get Billy up here. Now try to help me pull. The trail is smooth leading up here so he should slide up all right. Now let's pull."

Chester couldn't help much but they finally got Billy up the ravine and on flat ground. His leg was bleeding more and Chester started to get sick when he noticed the bone sticking out through his pants. The first thing Charlie did was find a piece of wood about two feet long from the old lean-to. It took him a while because most of the wood had become rotten over the years. He finally found a piece that he thought would work. He tossed the shovel away he used at the bottom of the ravine. It had worked to get Billy up on solid ground but it had somehow twisted and wasn't doing much good now. Charlie straightened Billy's leg and was glad he was out because he knew it must have been very painful.

"Chester, try and find me some long poles among all that old wood. I'll need some pretty strong ones. I'm going to try and make a travois to pull you two out of here. Can't think of another thing to do."

After going through all the old fragment of the lean-to Chester found a few strong pieces of wood. With pieces of the rope Charlie tied two of the longest pieces together at one end. He then tied shorter pieces in the middle section spreading them apart. Wider at the bottom and narrow at the top. Chester tried to help but stumbled around and fell several times. Finally, Charlie told him to just sit down somewhere.

Charlie felt bone tired as he finished the travois. He noticed the sun getting low in the West and thought he heard some night birds start they're calling out somewhere in desert. He thought how lonely this place appeared and then how close it must be to the man upstairs. It was pure, nothing artificial about this place. He could see why some men like to come out here and be with their thoughts. His thoughts were now of how he would manage to get both men back to civilization. If he could get them to the 4wheelers he could maybe use one of them to pull the travois the rest of the way. But getting them to the 4wheelers was going to be a job he didn't know he could handle.

The sun was almost down as he gathered what little fire wood Chester had pulled up. There were dried stumps and bushes of all kind of anything that would burn. It wasn't long until Charlie had a fire blazing and pulled Billy over next to it. Chester tried to talk but mumbled his words. He helped Chester find a place to lay down next to the fire and placed his sleeping bag over him. Billy was still out cold.

Charlie sat next to the fire, deep in his thoughts. He remembered how sometimes things would get hard between him a Betty when they were first married and she would have a talk with him. 'Now Charlie', she would say. 'This ain't nothing but a little bump in our road to happiness. I want you to be like the man I married. Strong, afraid of nothing and knew you could do anything you set your mind to. Now stop worrying about all this and just do your thing, as you use to say. The man upstairs will help you if you bog down. Now stop worrying and get to it.'

Charlie wiped a tear from his cheek as he gazed up into the beautiful sky full of glittering starts. There has to be something out there that will help me out of this mess. He poked the fire and sent sparks flying upward. God, he missed Betty.

CHAPTER THIRTEEN

Charlie had a small fire going before the sun came up. He spent a very restless night thinking of how he could accomplish such a task of pulling that piece of tied together wood back to the 4wheelers. The memories of his wife also kept him awake. The fire chased the morning chill away and warmed the left over coffee Charlie had placed on a rock beside the fire. Charlie checked all the bandages on Billy's leg and noticed him awake. He offered him some coffee. Billy shook his head sideways. He was quiet, not saying much. He groaned some when Charlie repositioned him closer to the fire.

Chester was doing great for an old man with a bullet hole in his shoulder. He sat up from his sleeping bag and said. "Don't you think we should get this show on the road, Charlie? We got a good way to go before we reach the 4wheelers. How's Billy looking? From here he don't look so good."

"Eat what's left to the jerky, Chester. We ain't got nothing else to take with us and you'll need all the strength you can muster."

Charlie helped Billy to the travois and placed him in the most comfortable place he could find on the crude object. As a last minute idea Charlie decided it might be a good idea to tie Billy in place. He drifted in and out of consciousness and mumbled to Charlie about not forgetting his thermos. Charlie grudgingly showed him the thermos and tied it next to him. Billy had just enough strength to grab it with his hand and held on to it like it was his life line. Chester tried to help but he stumbled around and almost fell several times. Charlie knew he couldn't be of much help, as he attached the man's back packs to the travois.

After Charlie was satisfied Billy was secured he walked to the front of the travois and attempted to pick up the long poles. Chester helped, but he was very shaky. As they got the contraption in place to pull Chester whispered to Charlie.

"Charlie, I had a bad dream last night. Anyway, I think it was a bad dream. I woke up and a big Mexican man was standing over us. He just watched, not doing anything. I started to shout out but I must have passed out. When I opened my eyes again he was gone."

Charlie had a strange look on his face. "Billy thought one of us walked around in the wet dirt the other night. Said there were foot prints in front of the cave entrance. I know either of us didn't it so I just brushed it off. Now I'm thinking maybe he did see a lot of foot prints, but there weren't any we put down. Remember all those reflections we keep seeing up in the mountain on our way in here? Those reflections could have been somebody keeping an eye on us, and then they came down to
our camp and did some checking. Don't like this, Chester. We're in something we ain't ever been in before. Now try to help me get this thing moving, we got to get Billy some help and I want out of here. I

ain't worried about you. I've seen worse things than that happen to your upper lip and you never stopped whistling. Ain't that right old man." Charlie smiled at Chester who was standing rather wobbly next to the travois. Now let's go."

Chester tried to help Charlie lift the long poles and get everything in position for moving. Charlie placed each pole under his arms on each side of himself where he could get a good grip. He slowly started to move forward pulling Billy with Chester walking beside him. The rocks were hard to dodge causing him to weave from side to side and slowed him down. Charlie knew they had to reach the 4 wheelers before night fall. They did not bring any camping gear with them but left it because of the extra weight. In a few hours Charlie looked up at the sun and immediately knew they would not be at the 4wheelers by nightfall. His breath was heavy as he called Chester over to him.

"Chester help me put this thing down, I need some rest before I start again." Chester tried to help Charlie place the long poles on the ground but caused more trouble than help. Charlie dropped the travois the last few inches and it Jarred Billy. He moaned in pain when the travois touched the ground. Charlie could scarcely move he was so sore, but he knew Billy's bandages needed to be checked. Charlie rubbed his hands together trying to get the circulation back as he dropped to his knees and half crawled around to where Billy lay unconscious. His leg had started to swell and turn blue. The bleeding had stopped and the look of the wound appeared to be fairly good, as far as Charlie could tell. He was no doctor but he was doing as good as he could. Charlie looked over to where Chester stood and noticed him lying on the ground. Very slowly Charlie crawled over to where Chester was stretched out on his back with his arms resting on his chest. He was breathing hard and whimpered somewhat. He looked up at Charlie and smiled.

"Got myself in a pickle brother. Don't know if I can go on or not. How much further to the 4wheelers you reckon?" Charlie didn't say a word as he untied and checked the bandage around Chester's arm.

"We've always been straight with each other, Chester. Don't think we can make it by night fall. Your wound looks good, so what's your problem old man?" Charlie was trying to get Chester mad. He had seen him do things no one else could do when he became angry. Maybe it would get him fired up he would be able to make it to the 4wheelers.

Chester looked up at Charlie, a frown on his face. "Now you listen to me, Charlie. I'm a few years older than you and it's starting to show. Someday you will be where I'm at in age and you'll slow down too, just like I am. I'm tired, Charlie, bone tired. I miss my daughter's front porch, her cooking and everything I thought I hated when I started this adventure. Don't know if I can go on. I'm sorry to let you down old buddy but I've reached my last mile. You always said, we ride together and we die together. This could be the time old partner." Chester rolled over and closed his eyes.

Charlie tumbled over beside him and rested in the sand. He thought about what Chester said. After all they had been through this was no way to end it. He'd like to be back in his room at the nursing home too. Anything but out here in the middle of the desert with two hurt friends and him pulling a travois. He thought about who would find them if they just died right here and now. His mind drifted to his wife and he smiled. He wondered if he would see her again and if so maybe death wouldn't be so bad. He could almost feel his arms around her. His eyes were growing heavier and heavier and he could not hold them open. When they closed his mind was blank. The sun cast a long shadow from a mesquite bush over the three as they laid motionless. From under the mesquite bush a rattle snake slithered through the sand and headed straight toward the men. The snake slowly squirmed over Billy and then went to Chester. He was somehow interested in Chester's arm. The snake coiled in a perfect circle on his chest and looked him in the eye. The snake had found a warm place to spend the night. In a matter of minutes, the darkness of the desert covered them and with it the chill of the night.

Out of the darkness an object moved toward the men. It walked very slow. The snake seemed to sense the presence of the object and slithered off into the bushes.

CHAPTER FOURTEEN

The hot morning sun on Charlies face forced him to open his eyes. It was a struggle but he finally pried them open. With one hand he rubbed his face trying to make sure he had any feeling. His face felt numb. Charlie looked over and observed Chester, who was on his back making strange noises through his nose. They were so tired when they collapsed last night the sleeping bags were never removed from the travois.

Charlie attempted to stand up and found it more difficult than he bargained for. His shoulders and back felt like someone had stuck a knife in it. Pain shot from one shoulder to the next. He let out a yell and fell on his knees, which startled Chester.

"What's going on here," shouted Chester as he started to move? He detected Charlie out of the corner of his eye. "What you doing down here on your hands and knees. You praying?"

Charlie moaned a sorrowful sound and looked at Chester. "I happened to be in this position because I fell down. I fell down because I'm so sore I can't hardly stand up." Both men were silent for a few minutes, like they are trying to catch their breath. Finally, Charlie forced himself up and it was about the same as the other day. Not good, but not bad. He knew it wouldn't be long until infection set in and then it would be too late to save his leg. He had to get him to a hospital fast. He glanced back to Chester. That old man used to be able to do anything he set his mind to do. He's so empty headed I doubt he ever knows the trouble we're in. If he could just help me with this travois we might make it in time to save Billy's leg.

Charlie worked the kinks out of his body and walked toward the travois. "You think you could help me get this in position to pull?"

Chester struggled to his feet and half stumbled and half walked over to

Charlie. "Don't guess we got anything to eat, now do we?"

"No, Chester, we ain't got anything to eat. Now let's get going."

"It sure would be nice if we had some coffee before we started," whispered Chester under his breath.

They lifted the travois up and Charlie grabbed hold. He let out a moan and got it in position. Chester stepped back and said, "I'd help you if I could Charlie, you know that."

"I know Chester, I know."

For an instant Charlie could see Chester in his youth, sitting on his Harley waiting for him to hurry up and let's go. Chester was always in a hurry and would say let's go all the time. He never slowed down. When he was leading on a motorcycle trip he would consistently ride faster than he should, just to see if Charlie could keep up with him. Charlie would invariably stay on his rear bumper just to show him he could not run off and leave him. Now look at him. An old man who can hardly stand up and has a bullet hole in him. My, have we changed, thought Charlie.

The pain in his shoulders suddenly exploded when he struggled with the travois to move forward. The weight seemed heavier today than yesterday. He paused for a moment, staring at a place on the ground. "Chester, did you get up last night and walk around some?"

Chester still trying to find his legs looked over at Charlie like he was crazy. "Yeah, I ran all around the place last night. Had to get my exercise in before breakfast. You must still think I'm the twisted blue steel you remember me by. Heck, Charlie, I can't hardly even stand up. No way I could walk around last night."

Charlie called him over to where he was holding the travois. "Take a look at the ground over there," Charlie motioned with his head over beside a mesquite bush.

Chester half way stumbled to where Charlie pointed. He stood still and breathed heavy. Taking deep breathes. "Charlie, we ain't alone out here. Someone was walking among us last night. I know it wasn't Billy, he can't even wake up. I don't like this partner. Not one bit."

Charlie repositioned his load with the long poles of the travois and shook his head. "Whatever it is, or whoever it is I wish he would leave us some water. It's going to be a long day and it looks like a hot one too. We got to get moving Chestier. We can't do anything about those tracks now."

With that said Charlie started pulling the travois. It was slow, but he finally managed to get it moving. Billy started thrashing around and making moaning sounds. The movement must have brought him out of his unconscious state. Chester walked beside him and tried to talk, but Billy acted like he couldn't hear.

"You been hurt, Billy. We're trying to get you some help. Charlie is pulling your sorry ass, so shut up." Chester told him in not to friendly manner. Charlie couldn't help but giggle at Chester.

The way Charlie figured it the 4wheelers must be right over the next sand hill. He didn't know how much father he could go. The memory of those rocks piled up in a special way kept running through Charlies mind. They had to have marked something. What could it have been?

The jagged rocks protruding from the desert that Billy tried to avoid with his 4wheeler were almost gone and the ground became smooth again. Charlie noticed the clouds forming up in the West and knew what that could mean. It wasn't long until the sound of thunder roared through the desert. It was always louder when a person's out in the middle of nowhere. The temperature suddenly dropped and the air felt like lead, not even a speck of breeze to cool a person off. Chester looked over at Charlie, he knew what they were in store for. Chester's legs were almost gone and he struggled to just keep up. He had found a piece of mesquite wood he tried to use as a crutch but he said it hurt his shoulder more than it helped him. Charlie pushed on trying to avoid the pain in his back and shoulder. Sometimes it was more than he could stand and he would fight to hold back his tears. If only Betty could be here she would keep him going. The only thing that kept him moving was the thought of his wife and how much he would like to be with her and not in the middle of this forsaken land.

The sun was now covered with the darkness of the storm clouds as they rolled and tumbled in strikes of lightning and thunder. It finally reached the men as it poured down in sheets of water. The poles of the travois started bogging down in the wet sand and made the pulling for Charlie almost impossible. At one time Charlie stumbled and fell far forward in the wet ground. As he tried to stand he noticed something appeared through the sheets of rain. He blinked his eyes and then wiped them with his arm. He looked over at Chester and he too was frozen with wonder as they both stared at the head of a horse studying them through the sheets of rain.

CHAPER FIVETEEN

The horse appeared on Chester's side and he moved as fast as he could to Charlies side. In doing so he fell in the mud. Charlie didn't offer to help him and Chester pulled himself by using the pole of the travois. He gazed through the rain at the horse and then at Charlie. "What in the world is a horse doing out here?"

Charlie couldn't hold the travois any longer and dropped it. Billy started moaning and trying to get off. He was coming out from his unconsciousness. The horse moved closer and turned sideways to the men. Someone was on the horse and then it suddenly disappeared as fast as the men had seen it. Charlie thought he heard laugher coming through the rain. He couldn't hold his head up any longer and collapsed on the ground. Chester fell on top of him.

Charlie struggled to get up. His emotional state of mind had suddenly changed. He pushed Chester off and stood up "Chester did you see what I think we saw? If you did there is someone out here with us and they look like they ain't going to help us any. If I was betting man I'd say Billy has something to do with this."

Charlie became mad for the first time. Maybe it was the image of someone on a horse or maybe the sun had finally got to him. He looked down at Billy with flame in his eyes. "Billy, you caused all of this. If it hadn't been for your, whatever you call it stuff, we would not be in this predicament."

Charlie reached down and untied the thermos bottle that held the pellets of rhodium. This caused Billy to really open his eyes. Charlie showed him the thermos and shouted. "Is this worth our life, and Chester's too? Is it that important that you risk your own life for it. My God man you've got a successful business, everything looks like it's going great for you and you want more. I used to work for some lawyers like you. All they wanted is more and more. Can't you see you can't take it with you Billy?"

Billy was wide awake now and tried to wipe away the rain on his face. With one hand he pulled at the rope holding him down. He started screaming as he watched Charlie open the top of the thermos and started pouring the contents out on the ground. The water runoff from a nearby sand mound caused a small stream of water and the rhodium landed in the middle of the run off.

"No, Charlie. Don't do that. I need the money. My business is about to go broke. This is the only way I can save it. Don't do this."

Charlie slowly poured the rhodium out and watched it drift away in the water. Billy shouted as loud as he could and calling him every name he could think of. Chester started laughing. "You're my man, Charlie Wise. You did the right thing. Never did like Billy in the first place."

Billy crawled off the travois and tried to save some of the rhodium but it was impossible. Charlie and Chester both laughed at him as he pulled himself on one leg through the mud and sheets of rain. Billy tried to stand and as he did he grabbed Charlie by the shirt and brought him down with him. Charlie found himself in a struggle as Billy tried to place Charlies face in the sandy water. Both were weak as babies and neither could get the advantage of the other.

"I'm going to kill you Charlie Wise. I never liked you in the first place. You treated me like dirt when I was growing up. I always looked up to you and you pushed me aside. This time I'm going to give you what you deserve." Billy kept hitting Charlie in the back of his head with his fist. Charlie couldn't breathe with his face buried in the water. Billy had managed to overpower Charlie and held him face down. Chester hurried to the side where the fight was going on and hit Billy over the head with his piece of mesquite wood he was using for a cane. Billy fell to the ground.

"That's enough of this crap Billy. I don't care what we did years ago. We should worry about what we need to do now. I want you to grow up and for once act like a man," shouted Chester.

The sudden out bust of energy by all three men caused them to instantly feel faint and start breathing hard. Chester fell to the ground and struggled to get his breath. Charlie rolled over from under Billy and started clearing the mud from his face. Billy laid on his stomach moaning with pain. He somehow managed to loosen the bandage on his leg which started bleeding again. All three men lay on the ground and let the rain pour down on them.

In time the rain stopped and the sun burned through the black clouds bringing with it the heat of the desert. Chester moved first, and then Charlie. Billy was the last to wake and when he did his groan was loud and painful. All three men were weak from exhaustion and moved slow as they tried to stand, all but Billy. He pulled himself up on his one knee and rested against the pole of the travois. They all caught a glimpse of the strange object beside them at the same time. All were too feeble to do anything but stare at a man on a horse watching them. Charlie spoke first.

"Who are you stranger? What do

you want? Can you help us?"

The man backed up his horse so he could have a better look at the three men on the ground. "No, I will not help you. You are adversaries of my family and the many men that lost their lives on this hunk of wasted land you call the desert. I have promised my mother and my grandmother to never help anyone why comes on this land. It is a lifeless land that holds many memories of killings of my family and friends."

Charlie, Chester and Billy all looked at each other like they didn't know what to do. The man talking to them was dressed like an old time cowboy, he carried a gun on each hip and one in his saddle. His clothes were of the kind the Mexicans wore, bright colored long sleeve shirt with stitching on the sleeves and back. His hat was large like the Mexican ranchers wore. Long black hair hung out from under his hat. He was a mean looking man.

"We ain't killed anyone out here. We just need some help," shouted Chester.

"I have said, that I cannot do. I will

tell you if you are trying to get to the machines you call 4wheeler, they are just over that ridge." He pointed toward an elevation in the desert about a mile from them. "I think you can make it if you try hard and not start fighting between yourselves."

As he rode off he stopped like he had forgotten something, turned around and tossed a water canteen to the ground where Charlie, Chester and Billy were. "I will give you some water. You look like you could use some."

Charlie picked up the canteen and in a weak voice asked him. "Before you leave please tell us who you are and where you come from?"

The man turned around in his saddle, pushed his hat back and took a deep breath. "Long time ago this land belonged to two very nasty men named Washington and Hightower. They tried to raise cattle out here but did not know anything about raising cattle They took to robbing people. Many times, cowboys from my family ranch which is across the river, would come over here looking for stray cattle and would end up being shot by these two men. We had several battles with them and finally decided it was not worth losing any more men for this piece of God for taken land. If some of our cattle wondered here, so be it. That was years ago, back in my grandfather's days. We have always treated this land as a place of evil. I happen to see you a few days ago start your adventure out here and just had to find out what you were doing. I see now you were doing nothing. I wish you luck in finding your machines that will take you to the comfort of your lives. Let this be a warning not to come out here again." With that he turned and rode off.

CHAPTER SIXTEEN

Charlie was able to get Billy back on the travois and half way tied him so he wouldn't fall off if he passed out. Chester still tried to walk beside the travois but found it almost impossible. Charlie knew he wouldn't last much longer. All the men had thoughts of who the Mexican man was that gave them the water but kept their opinions to themselves. The water given to them by the stranger saved them. Charlie pressed on but it was slow moving. The desert heat started taking its toll and he doubted he could go much further.

The topped the sand hill the stranger had pointed to and sure enough the 4wheelers were there still covered with the bush where they had hidden them from view. Charlie moved slow as he pulled the brush from one the 4wheelers. Chester tried but kept falling down. It was then Charlie knew he would not be able to ride one of the 4wheelers and that would be another problem.

Charlie used some of the rope holding the travois together to strap the long poles to the back luggage rack of the 4wheeler. Billy never did move and Charlie started to worry it might be too late for him, he could lose his leg. Chester rested in a shade of a tall mesquite tree trying to hold his eyes open. He looked wasted. Charlie pulled on the polls to make sure they would hold. When he felt satisfied they were secured he called Chester over.

"Chester, you can't make it any further, you're going to have to ride back here with Billy"

Chester slowly crawled over to the travois and attempted to position himself. He looked up a Charlie with desperate eyes and said, "Charlie, looks like it's all up to you to get us out of here. We can say we had another great adventure, can't we, partner?"

"We sure can, Chester. We're

gonna laugh about all this as we sit on your daughter's porch drinking lemonade."

Chester started to laugh but broke out in a dry cough. Charlie retrieved the water canteen he had strapped to the travois and offered Chester a drink. Chester shook his head as to say, I don't need any. Charlie knew how tough this old man could be and hung it back on the pole. He examined Billy again before taking off toward the truck. When he removed the bandage, it didn't look good at all. It appeared to be festering with several pockets of white pus accumulating around where the bone had protruded from his leg. Charlie knew time was important, he had to hurry. The sun was almost down and darkness soon covered them as Charlie cranked the 4wheeler and started off toward where he thought Billy had left the truck.

The bright moon light helped Charlie find his way across the desert floor. The head light on the 4wheeler didn't assist much. Only a small spot in front of them was illuminated by the miniature head light. Charlie rubbed his face to try and stay awake. His eyes were heavy and felt like there was sand in them. He had to get to the truck.

Charlie topped a small sand hill and for some reason he looked to his right. He suddenly sensed his body drifting in space and not feeling anything, His body felt numb. Right off his right side a dim light beamed through the darkness. In the middle of this radiation he could see his wife's face. She smiled at him and said in an unworldly voice that seemed to titillate his ears.

"Charlie you've been in worse situations than this and always came out on top. Remember when you broke your foot on your motorcycle and had to crawl to that house off to the side of the road. You told me you almost cried it hurt so bad. You made it, just like you can make it to the truck too. Just believe in yourself and you can do it Charlie. Don't give-up" The light slowly faded away.

Charlie blinked his eyes but never slowed down. Was this a dream or is she really talking to him? He was confused and somewhat scared of what happened. He slowed down and reached back for the water. He poured it over his head and rubbed his face. How much longer could he go on. He was so tired he could be seeing things that were not there. Or were they. He started again. This time driving faster than he should.

The morning sun brought a chill to Charlies body. Although the sun was warm it appeared to generate a tingling through his arms and legs. He had to stop and walk around. He pulled up in a sandy piece of smooth ground and slowly crawled off the machine. The first thing he did was check on Chester. He was doing great for an old man with a bullet in his arm. Chester gradually opened his eyes when the 4wheeler stopped. He stared at Charlie through blood shot eyes and said. "We at the truck yet?"

"Not yet Chester. It won't be long."

Charlie opened the water canteen and held it to Chester's lips. He gradually managed to swallow some and pushed it away with his good arm. "Don't need any now Charlie. Let's keep it for an emergency,"

"This is an emergency, Chester, now drink some more water. Your body needs it." Chester tried to take more water but had a hard time doing so. He just didn't want any more. Charlie checked on Billy again and shock his head, Billy was getting worse. Charlie then tried to stretch his arms and legs to get the blood circulating again. When he felt better he gradually climbed back on the 4wheeler and started in the direction of where he thought the truck to be located.

The truck had to be close. Everything looked like it did when they unloaded the 4wheelers. It just had to be over the next sand hill. When Charlie topped a rise, he could see in the distance an object that he thought was the truck. His vision was blurry and he rubbed his eyes to try and clear them. Still it looked hazy in the distance. The suns heat rays danced up and around the metal object causing it to cast back an unfocused image. Charlie headed straight for it. We're going to make it. We're going to make it, we're going to make it, kept pulsating through Charlies head. Almost there.

His idea was to place Billy in the back seat of the truck. He was glad Billy had a two seater pick up. Chester could sit up front with me and help me drive if needed. It had been years since Charlie drove a car but he knew he could make it to the highway. He could then flag down help. It's going to work, we're going to make it.

Charlies thoughts were destroyed when he pulled up beside the truck. He couldn't believe what sat in front of him. All the doors were opened and it had been gutted. The seats were gone. The tires were gone. There was just a skeleton of what used to be a beautiful truck. Charlie almost cried as he walked toward it. What can he do now? Can he make it to the highway? Billy had warned them sometime people from across the river see things and come over to steal them. This had to be what happened.

Charlie looked out over the vast desert surrounding him and let his head fall against his chest and closed his eyes. He needed rest in the worse way. The heat from the sun felt like it never had before.   He dosed off sitting on the machine. He suddenly woke up when the heat of the sun on his face became unbearable.   He heard a sound that brought a chill to him. It was the rattle of a snake. He jumped off the 4wheeler and almost tumbled to the ground he was so sore. A rattle snake was coiled and preparing to strike Billy's good leg that was hanging off the travois. Charlie looked down and found a rock which he'd grabbed and threw at the snake. The snake slithered off behind a bush. Charlie fell down face first on the sand. He was exhausted.

CHAPTER SEVENTEEN

Tom Doss, a driver for Safeway groceries was making his last run of the day over the lonely highway that ran down to Mexico. Sun appeared to be brighter today, thought Tom as he let the diesel purr and he sat back and smoked another cigarette. This job was a boring one but Tom felt lucky to have it. Suddenly he grabbed the steering wheel with both hands. Something appeared up in front of him about a hundred yards. He couldn't make it out but it sure looked out of place. Tom tossed his cigarette out the window and started gearing down. As he rolled closer he couldn't believe his eyes. It looked like a man on a 4wheeler pulling some kind of platform with two men laying on it. Tom had to lock up his brakes to keep from rolling past them. He got the big rig stopped and jumped out the door and ran back to see what this was all about.

He looked at the blood soaked bandages on the leg of Billy and on the arm of Chester. Tom didn't know what to say at first, and then asked if they needed any help. Charlie heard him and answered in a weak voice. "We're in pretty good shape, could we hitch a ride to the closest hospital?"

Tom didn't know what to say and suddenly turned and ran to his truck and reached in for the radio. "Breaker, breaker, we need an ambulance out here on the highway 12. I found three men that look like they're all broken up beside the road."

It had been two months since the boys talked. Chester was home with his daughter resting and doing good. He spent a lot of time on the front porch just thinking about what could have been if Charlie hadn't thrown out the stuff that supposedly was worth so much. He tried to get the thought of going to Mexico to retire out of his head, but he still had his dream.

Billy had received some very good doctoring and was able to save his leg but he would have to leave it in a cast for a long time. He hobbled around using a crutch and seemed like he was in good spirits as he crossed the showroom floor wishing everyone a good day. For some reason his business picked up and it was doing great. He thought how the rhodium could have helped him with the cash flow but in a way, he was glad he didn't need it. He pulled himself up, by himself, and didn't need any help.

Charlie moped around the nursing home for weeks. Not hardly talking to anyone but a yard boy who kept the grounds neat and trimmed. The nurses would see him all during the day following the yard boy around and talking to him. One of the nurses asked why he was so interested in that young boy.

"It has something to do with motorcycles. Charlie used to ride a Harley and anyone with a motorcycle he likes to talk to. I guess they tell each other how much fun they had on their bikes."

"That's probably right. You know how old men like to brag."

On a bright Saturday afternoon, the nursing home suddenly vibrated with the sounds of police sirens and policemen wanting talk to the nurses. Someone had stolen the yard boys' motorcycle. It was a big deal in the little town where everyone never locked their doors. The crime rate was so low some people questioned if they even needed a police force.

Nurse Smitty was the first to be questioned about the theft. "Did you know the yard boy very good?" asked a dumb looking policeman that wore his clothes way too tight. Guess he wanted to show off his muscles, thought Smitty.

"My gosh," answered the nurse. You would think someone got murdered around here. "No, I didn't know the yard boy that good. He's been working for us a long time, maybe a year or more. He did his job and didn't association with many of our residents."

"It would help us if you could tell us

who he talked to around here. They might know something that could help us recover his motorcycle."

"Well I guess his favorite was Mr. Wise. Charlie talks to everyone and one of our favorite residents. We all just love him." The Nurse turned to one of the assistants and asked her to go and get Charlie. She returned with a strange look on her face. "He's not in his room and no one around here has seen him today. Nurse Smitty had a look of surprise on her face. "That's very strange. He asked me to make him some sandwiches this morning. Said he didn't want to come in for lunch. He took a jug of water with him because he didn't want to get hot. I thought it was a little strange but then you have to know Charlie. He does a lot of strange things for an old man of his age. Just a few months ago he went on an adventure out in the desert with his old buddy. They almost didn't make it back."

The policeman wrote some notes in a book and closed it with a snap. "Would you contact us when you find this Charlie Wise. He might be able to help us." The policeman turned and walked away leaving the nurses standing in the hall.

"I can see why some people don't like the police now. They were very rude." The nurses turned to walk away when nurse Smitty called after them. "Let's all see if we can find Charlie. This is not like him. Hope he's all right."

A month went by with no sign of Charlie. His rent had been paid by a trust fund he set up years ago. They didn't know if they should let his room out to someone else or just wait for Charlie to come back. The police listed him as missing and an alert had been put out on him. The nurses were distressed about the Charlie Wise situation and the rumors were flying. Some thought he was kidnapped by the same people that stole the yard boys' motorcycle. And then maybe he caught them in the act of stealing it and trying to stop them and was hurt. It was the talk of the nursing home.

On another beautiful Saturday morning a delivery truck backed up to the door of the nursing home. Two burly men approached the front door. "We have a delivery for the nursing home. It goes to a woman named Dottie."

"Bring it in guys I'll make sure she gets it."

"You don't understand, Ma. It's rather heavy. You should tell us where you want it placed."

The nurse looked confused. "What in the world is it a piano?"

The men started laughing. "That's right ma'am, a piano for one of your residents named Dottie." The delivery man handed the nurse a packing slip. There was no return address only a note that read. 'Hope you enjoy it, Dottie.'

Billy Tate wobbled across the show room floor on his crutch as a secretary followed him. "Mr. Tate, this came registered mail for you. I signed for it." She handed it to Billy and he opened it and money fell to the floor. A smile came across his face. "Hope this is enough for the supplies we used, I added a little more for the hardship, Hope you learned your lesson." Billy walked slowly to his office and sat down behind his desk. He took a deep breath and whispered. "Charlie, I learned more than you'll ever know. You and Chester will always be my best friends."

Chester was bored rocking in the chair on his daughter's porch but he had made up his mind that was all there was left in life. He had his memories, and there were plenty of them. He laughed to himself at some of the unbelievable things he and Charlie did in their youth. Chester was almost asleep when a special delivery man walked up to the porch.

"Looking for a Mr. Chester Marble."

Chester snapped out of his dose and jumped up. Someone is writing to him, wonder who it could be. He signed the form and took the letter and carefully opened it. Like savoring the moment. A piece of paper fell out onto the floor of the porch. He reached down and picked it up before reading the letter. It was a bus ticket to a place in Mexico he couldn't even pronounce. His hand started to shake as he read the letter.

At the very top of the page a hundred dollars bill was paper clipped to the paper. He started reading very slowly. "Chester, I went back and found the mother lode. It wasn't rhodium that was buried under that strange pile of rocks I told you about. I'll explain it all to you when you get here. There's a ticket and some spending money. Come to the address written below and we can chase all the pretty girls together. If we can't ride together anymore we can die together. See you soon."

Chester's eyes started watering and he let out a yell. His dream of going to Mexico could come true. He told himself you're never too old to dream.

In a small Mexican bar Charlie enjoyed his Coke. He never did like the last of whiskey. He was wearing a bright cooler shirt, not buttoned at the top anymore like he used to ware. He wore cutoffs and sandals and enjoyed the company of all the girls around him. They all liked to mother him and take care of him. He didn't look like the old Charlie from the nursing home. His face showed happiness. The wrinkles of worry were gone and the smile of contentment seem to light up the dim bar. Suddenly the doors opened and the bright sun beamed into the room. Chester slowly walked in and recognized Charlie at the bar. He walked over and shook his head as he started so smile. Charlie stood up and put his arms around him. They embraced and started laughing.

YOUR NEVER TO OLD TOO
ENJOY LIFE.

ABOUT THE AUTHOR

Grady lives in Hurst, Texas with his wife, Jan and their little dog, Dolly. When he's not writing another book he enjoys riding his Harley with his friends and gathering inspiration for another book.